Za

and the
Secret of Gloomwood Forest

By Keira Gillett

ISBN-13: 978-1-942750-01-7

Library of Congress Control Number: 2015905663

Dedication:

I dedicate this book to my mother who instilled the love of reading in me at an early age. Thanks for being my best friend.

To Readers:

Zaria Fierce was a little kernel of an idea that kept popping to life. I knew her long before I knew her story… or for that matter the villain. Her story started three times and was abandoned twice for another plot. She might have gone to a school for misfit fairy tale creatures, or she might have run away from a dastardly plot to take over her kingdom. But that wasn't her story and she let me know it. I hope as you are reading this book (and viewing the illustrations) you are swept away by the fantasy and adventure. Enjoy!

Table of Contents:

Prologue: A Mouse's Introduction

A timid thing was Zaria Fierce. The antithesis of her last name, the young girl was shy, quiet, and self-contained. She kept to her own company most of the time, as she and her family often moved due to her adoptive father's military career. Because of his new post, the family was stationed in Norway.

The move to Fredrikstad was recent, only ten days ago. Zaria would be starting at another new school soon. This would be her fourth school in four years.

She hadn't made any friends yet – not seeing any children in their building – but it was okay, because like her adoptive mom, Meredith (Merry), who was a dedicated housewife and online professor, Zaria preferred reading to almost any other activity.

Fantasy was her favorite genre, because the worlds were so much more vibrant and exciting than ordinary tales. They featured giants, fairies, pixies, ogres, brownies, trolls, banshees, witches, wishes, curses, and so much more. "Why be ordinary when you could be extraordinary?" she often wondered.

Zaria loved the Colonel. Not only was he an attentive father, doting on Zaria with the books she adored, he was also the bravest, most courageous person Zaria knew. She often wished she had his self-possession and cool levelheadedness. If she did, she just knew her life would take her on an adventure like those of the heroes and heroines in her books.

Her new school was six blocks from their rented apartment. She could walk it easily and often did in the first two weeks with her mom. They both loved crossing a quaint pedestrian bridge two blocks from the school with its ornate metal scrollwork featuring curlicues, spirals, and swirls. To them both it seemed enchanting and special.

As lovely as the walks were, Zaria was ready to go it alone and perhaps meet up with a few of the children on her route. So on Monday, at the start of the third week of school, she kissed her mom on the cheek, made assurances to text her safe arrival, and dashed out the door, carrying her latest book on Norwegian fairy tales, and her lunch.

What Zaria and her parents didn't know was that it wasn't by accident that the Colonel was stationed in Norway. The clock was ticking down – had been since they arrived in Norway – and someone was watching and waiting, eager and expectant. Change was imminent and magic joined the bite of fall in the air. Zaria would get her wish for adventure sooner than she expected.

Chapter One: The Scrollwork Bridge

Two weeks later, Zaria found herself running to catch up with her Chinese friend Christoffer who was jogging a block ahead of her. The wind caught at her scarf and whipped the ends of it and her hair into her face. She was running a little late today, because her mom insisted on fussing a little extra for her birthday. Zaria's dark hair had been freshly braided before the wind snagged it. She wore a crisp red bow jauntily secured over her right ear and a new woolen dress, also red, with a black winter coat that hung to the backs of her knees.

"Christoffer, will you stop running and let me catch up?" Zaria shouted, pounding the pavement and juggling her backpack, books, and lunch.

"Can't!" he called back, with a grin, over his shoulder. "Someone was very late this morning. I waited as long as I could, but you know I can't be late. Mum's the teacher. I have to set a good example. She's going to be livid if I'm late. Hurry up!"

Zaria puffed along behind him for another minute, but gave up as he crossed the scrollwork bridge and turned the corner. She was willing to take the tardy. She secured her bag and books. Then she straightened her hair, tucked flyaways back into their proper place, and tugged at her dress and coat, making sure everything was properly arranged. "Stupid, Christoffer," she muttered as she started walking again.

At the bridge, Zaria once again admired the intricate metal scrolling that made up the rails. She ran her gloved hand gently over the top, listening to her feet land on the wooden planks with a steady clop, clop, clop. The river twinkled in the muted morning light – the only creatures to disturb its smooth surface were a family of swans. As she watched them, they honked in agitation and took flight, spoiling the peaceful setting.

"Morning, Princess," came a raspy voice ahead of her. Zaria glanced up from the swans and jerked in surprise.

In the middle of the bridge, crouched on the rail, was a brown creature dressed in rags. It had overly big ears which were the same size as its head and a long nose. Its mouth held a perpetual frown, pulled in a grimace. When it attempted a smile, it revealed yellow teeth. Zaria rubbed her eyes to erase the strange image. Except it didn't erase, it moved closer.

"Princess be lacking manners," it said, wiping a gnarled hand across its nose, sniffing loudly. "Won't matter if you be mannered or not in the end. Taste all the same to me."

"What are you?" Zaria asked worriedly, clutching her backpack, toying with the zipper.

If she could get into her backpack she could grab her mobile and call her mom. Was this a joke? Christoffer's mum was going to be the least of his problems when Zaria caught up with him. This was not funny.

"Ignorant and mannerless. Tsk. I be the river's guardian," the man-like creature stated, pointing to himself with slightly webbed fingers. "You may call me Olaf, if you be liking."

A shaft of light lit him up, revealing that his brown skin was leathery in parts and scaly in others. The scales glinted a muted, muddy blue-brown. He scratched his chin, and then moved closer. Silently, he slipped off the rail and straightened to full height, revealing a tall body and long lanky limbs.

Zaria took a step back, feasting her eyes on Olaf. He reminded her of creatures in her books, but uglier. He was definitely not human. Maybe Christoffer had nothing to do with Olaf's presence. That meant she was either dreaming or stumbling into her very own story. A dash of excitement filled her belly.

"Do you grant wishes?" she asked with eager anticipation, letting the zipper of her backpack go.

"Wishes?" Olaf asked incredulously. "Wishes? Bah!" he laughed. "My stomach be wishing for fresh meat. It's been far too long. Come here Princess, and let me eat you."

The excitement in Zaria's belly vanished instantly, replaced with a cold slither of fear.

"Eat me?" she squeaked.

Olaf nodded. "I be very hungry."

"Oh well. I can see how that would be tempting," Zaria said, scrambling for an alternative. Her scattered thoughts landed on the fairy tale of *The Three Billy Goats Gruff*. She breathed a little easier. Straightening up she said, "But I'm only a child, I am not fattened up."

"Nay," Olaf said wickedly, his mouth stretching into an awkward smile. "I've watched you for weeks, Princess. You kept crossing my waters, over this very bridge, protected by your youth. Today be your thirteenth birthday though, be it not? You not be protected anymore."

The situation was worse than she feared. He'd been watching her? How had she not noticed? "H-h-how did you know?"

"I can smell it. Princess, you have the sweetest blood of all. You will be tender… tender and juicy…."

"Don't come any closer, p-p-pervert," she stammered.

Zaria scrambled back on the bridge, and Olaf stopped his advancement, eyeing her with bemusement. That look was definitely worse than when Olaf looked at her hungrily. She would not be eaten. She refused to let it happen, but Olaf was fearsome, and he terrified her with his calm demeanor.

"Pervert? Princess, it be not nice to be calling trolls names." He stepped toward her again, hands loose at his sides, and sharp eyes trained on her. "It not do you any good to run. I be collecting my toll from you Princess, whether you be interested in paying it or not."

"Did I say I wouldn't pay it?" Zaria asked. She forced a laugh out, noticing that her voice was high-pitched and squeaky. "I'm happy to pay it, only – only, today isn't the best day to do it. I'm expected at school on the other side of the bridge. I must get there before my absence is noticed."

"Why be Olaf care? After I eat you, Princess, you be missing anyway."

How had the goats managed to trick the troll? This was harder than she thought. Unzipping her bag Zaria searched for her phone feeling frantic. She did not want to be on the bridge one moment more than she had to be.

Latching on to his nickname for her like it was a lifeline Zaria gasped, "Because as a princess, I must have subjects."

She relaxed, but still she searched for the phone. She could play this game and possibly even win it. Clearly he thought she was important and wasn't smart enough to know better. Perhaps she could trick him after all.

"Princess be having lots of subjects. Again, why be Olaf care?"

"You're hungry. I will send you a feast. It's as the human proverb goes: give a man a fish, and he's fed for a day; teach a man to fish, and he's fed for life. If you eat me, you would be hungry again in a day. If you wait, I can ensure you're fed for a year."

Olaf tilted his head, bringing a crooked hand to his rounded chin, pondering the offer. Zaria held her breath, ready to flee at a moment's notice.

"How tell I if you be telling the truth, Princess?"

Zaria bit her lip nervously. "Are you asking if I have honor?"

"Yes," he hissed. "I wonder if Princess be having honor, as you not be having manners or intelligence."

Zaria bristled. "I have honor. Let me pass freely across the river, and I will do as I say."

Over the next few breaths she and Olaf played a cat-and-mouse game. He'd move toward her; she'd move back. He stopped again, and she'd still. Then he would move again and start it over. Finally, he narrowed his eyes.

"If you be lying, Princess, I not be taking it kindly. I shall let you pass, but I not be waiting more than three days for you to fulfill your promise."

Zaria nodded, eager to agree and get away. "I will keep my promise."

He glowered menacingly. "If you not be keeping your word, I be seeking retribution as befitting the crime. Do you understand?" Zaria nodded again, but the troll was not convinced. "Speak up," he growled.

"Yes, I understand," Zaria said meekly.

"Three days," Olaf warned and slinked over the bridge.

She expected to hear a splash, but as Zaria raced to the edge of the railing and looked over all she saw were concentric ripples radiating outward. The swans which had flown away at the appearance of the troll, glided back into view and settled calmly on the waters. The troll was well and truly gone. She'd done it; she'd tricked the troll. She nearly whooped in glee.

But as the swans continued to swim lazily, Zaria frowned. They were unruffled by the series of events, as if their morning hadn't been disrupted. Had she hallucinated the whole event? No. She had a vivid imagination, but nothing quite like this had ever happened before when she day-dreamed.

There had been a troll! Right here in Norway, just like her books. She shook her head in disbelief, hiked up her bag, and dashed across the bridge and the rest of the way to school. Nobody was going to believe her, if she said she was desperately late because of a bridge troll. It was definitely worse than saying the dog ate your homework. And, Zaria didn't have a dog.

***

Unhappily, Zaria was right that nobody would believe her. When she got to school she was singled out and given after-school detention, despite her story of being stopped on the bridge. Christoffer, too, had received a pink slip and would be joining her.

"Zaria," he hissed when she sat down. "Who stopped you on the bridge? I didn't see anyone."

"I think it was a troll."

"Like from your fairy tales?" Christoffer questioned skeptically, his brown eyes crinkling at the corners. Then he brightened. "Maybe someone was dressed up for Cosplay."

"N-n-no," Zaria shook her head in the negative. "Definitely not. It was a troll, troll. Big ears, big nose, string-bean thin, dressed in rags. Ugly. Very ugly."

"A vaga–"

"Mr. Johansen," Mrs. Johansen called from the front of the room. "Just what are you talking about with Miss Fierce that is more important than history class?"

That shut the two of them up instantly. Zaria ducked behind her text book, as Christoffer tried to brazen it out with a cheeky grin. His mother gave him a warning glare. Zaria did not envy Christoffer in that moment. He would be getting a lecture tonight on proper behavior.

Now, the consequences of angering a troll are not to be dismissed as insignificant. For Zaria, who saw neither hide nor hair of Olaf over the next three days, assumed she'd been mistaken about the encounter. After all, a troll in the middle of modern-day Norway was extremely unlikely.

The first night she'd been wound up and jittery. She tried to tell Merry about it after school, but her mother thought she was talking about a book and told her to go do her homework. Then, her father laughed at her even more boisterous retelling of the event over dinner and birthday cake. While slicing a second slice for himself and for her, he agreed with his wife that it was a fine tale and told her she should keep working on it.

After that conversation, Zaria was confused. Olaf had looked run-down and dressed in rags. Maybe he had been a homeless old man and not a troll at all. Could she have made the whole thing up? But Zaria didn't consider herself to be someone to cry wolf over nothing. Olaf had to be real.

When dinner was over, her parents showered her with a small mound of presents, including a new fantasy book series she was most eager to read. They stayed up as a family and watched one of Zaria's favorite movies, *The Labyrinth.* She loved the puppetry and puzzles that needed to be solved in the maze.

Then it was time for bed. Zaria trudged upstairs with her goodies, determined to find out if she'd read the scene with Olaf in her Norwegian fairy tale book. She pored over its contents until her eyes got blurry and heavy with sleep. That is how the Colonel found her when he came to tuck her into bed. He urged her into bed and reached to turn off the lights.

"Night, pumpkin," he murmured as she drifted off to sleep.

In her dreams, Zaria met with Olaf again and again. Each time the bridge troll's appearance seemed a little less real and little more like meeting a puppet from *Jim Henson's Creature Shop…* until when it was morning, Zaria was certain that the truth was that she met a homeless man and conjured up a different scenario to make it seem a little less scary.

She asked her mother to accompany her to school for the remainder of the week as a precaution. Merry didn't mind and made it special by stopping for breakfast from a neighborhood bakery. Together they ate delicious puff pastries and drank hot chocolate, breathing in the moist steamy air, and warming their reddened noses. Zaria was so delighted with this early morning routine she never hesitated at the scrollwork bridge and soon forgot Olaf completely.

Chapter Two: Her Loyal Subject

Zaria spent the weekend with her nose buried in her new book series, sequestered away in a cozy reading nook piled high with pillows and blankets. On Sunday, Merry served her lunch on a breakfast tray. The comforting smell of chicken and vegetable soup made Zaria's mouth water. Paired with fresh bread from the bakery, it was without a doubt her favorite meal. The soup went down hot and thick. The red potatoes were soft and the peppers had just enough bite in them to give her a little zing.

She only had a few chapters left of the second book and she couldn't wait to see what happened to the lightning wielding magician and his misfit friends. Just as she was settling back into her reading, an urgent knock came at their front door. Zaria looked up to see her mom answering the door. She couldn't see who was there, and she couldn't hear what was said, but she did see her mom shake her head and say, "He isn't here."

Then Merry turned and motioned for Zaria to join her. Zaria closed her book with trepidation. What was going on? Her mom gathered her into a hug and pulled her forward.

Mrs. Johansen stood there, with a very serious expression on her face, beside a stroller with one of Christoffer's twin sisters inside. Her dark eyes were worried. She crouched low to be at Zaria's height and grabbed her hands with an urgency that made Zaria's heart thump painfully in her chest.

"Zaria, honey, have you seen Christoffer? Was he here yesterday?" Her voice trembled with barely contained emotion.

Zaria shook her head. "I haven't seen him since school on Friday. Why? What's going on?"

Mrs. Johansen stood up. She looked so bone weary even her thick dark ponytail drooped. "He said he was going out to play with one of his friends. He hasn't returned. The police only now began to look for him. They think he's run away. Did he mention anything to you that would make you think he would run off? Was he mad about the after-school detention on Monday?"

"No. We laughed it off. He seemed fine on Friday, when we parted after school. I haven't heard from him. Did you check with Filip or Aleks? Geirr?"

"Yes, I called them all last night. Zhuang is speaking with them now. But I thought that perhaps Christoffer might have come to you. Boys are funny about who they might speak to if there were problems. You're his only friend who is a girl. I was hoping…" Mrs. Johansen trailed off, inhaled deeply and fumbled for her purse on the back of the stroller. "I don't know why he would do this. Or, God forbid, if something happened to him." She pulled out a handkerchief and blew her nose.

Zaria felt hopeless. She didn't know anything that might be of help for Mrs. Johansen. "I'm sorry," she mumbled, looking down at her bare feet.

Merry briefly hugged her tighter and pushed her away. "It's okay, sweetheart. Why don't you go back to your room? I'm going to make me and Emma some tea."

***

Going to school Monday was awful. Zaria dragged her feet all the way. She missed Christoffer terribly and wished she knew what to do – how she could help. She kept her head down and her hands tucked into her pockets. Merry walked beside her in silence, equally lost in her own thoughts. They crossed the bridge and reached the school shortly thereafter.

Merry crouched and pulled Zaria into a fierce hug. "It's going to be okay, sweetheart. Christoffer will be found, and it will okay."

Zaria's eyes watered and she hid her face in Merry's neck, returning the hug equally fiercely. "I hope so, Mom."

Merry leaned back and wiped at Zaria's tears with her soft fuzzy gloves. "If you need to, call me and I'll come get you. We'll play hooky and go to a museum."

Zaria nodded and rushed off, just as the bell rang in the courtyard. Mrs. Johansen wasn't in the history classroom. A substitute stood at the board and introduced himself as Mr. Magnusdotter. He was tall, thin, and a few years past middle age. He had a large nose and wire rim glasses. His voice was kind, as he spoke with the children, explaining Mrs. Johansen's and Christoffer's absence.

He told them, if they remembered anything unusual or anything Mr. Johansen might have said to indicate where he was, to share it immediately. The school counselor was also mentioned in case any of the children felt anxious or needed to talk about their feelings.

The day went by interminably. The students were all hushed during classes and gossiping in whispers in the corridors. Filip – blond and green-eyed – and Aleks – a brown-eyed redhead with freckles – met Zaria at lunch. She'd never really spoken to them before today, but they were instantly bonded in the crisis over Christoffer. Together they solemnly went through the cafeteria line, saving their talking until they reached a back table.

Their black friend Geirr had gone home with a stomachache, which Zaria knew had nothing to do with what he ate for breakfast and everything to do with the lugubrious (but still expectant) atmosphere at school. All the children were watching them, waiting to see if they knew anything, and gossiping in whispers.

Aleks hunched his shoulders and glanced around at the faces watching them. He leaned in and whispered, "He didn't say anything to me. I wish he had. He could have spent the night. Mom and dad wouldn't have minded."

"Yeah," said Filip. "I don't know what he was thinking. Or not thinking. I know he didn't come to see me, we didn't have any plans."

"We didn't have plans either," Zaria said, poking at her meal. She really wasn't all that hungry.

"Same," Aleks said. He too was picking at his food, but he was making a better effort at eating it than Zaria. "You need to eat," he told her. "It doesn't do anyone any good if you make yourself sick."

She nodded and shoveled food into her mouth. It tasted like sawdust, and stuck in her throat. She hastily swallowed her milk. The next bite was better. And the next. Eventually, all three finished their meal and gathered their trash to toss in the bins by the cafeteria doors.

Aleks scratched the back of his neck. "Do you want to get together after school to look for him?"

Filip broke out into a smile. "That's a great idea! I bet we can think of loads of places where he might have gone."

"We should tell somebody before we go out though," Zaria fretted. "No point to making all of our parents anxious."

Aleks nodded. "Agreed. Let's meet up at my house and start from there."

They all agreed and arranged their plans for the afternoon before splitting off to their classes. Zaria was eager now for school to be over, not to escape the depressing atmosphere, but because she was keen to start the search for Christoffer.

***

Mr. Mickelsen, Aleks' dad, went with them on their search, which made Zaria's mother happy. Filip had told Geirr of the plans and the suddenly well boy joined them as they looked for Christoffer. Of them all, Geirr was the most optimistic. He was usually very reserved and straitlaced.

They searched their favorite hangouts around town and especially in the neighborhoods where they all lived. Christoffer wasn't to be found anywhere. Aleks' dad talked and tried to keep everyone's spirits up, but as the afternoon wore on, it became clear to the children that they weren't going to find their friend. Worse still was that there weren't any clues about where he might have gone. Nothing to give them hope.

When they got back to Aleks' place, his father clapped him and Filip on the shoulder and gripped them tight for a moment. "Something will come up, boys," he said and headed inside.

"This sucks," Geirr said, kicking at the pavement. "What now?"

Aleks scratched the back of his neck. "I don't know. I really don't. Why would Christoffer do this?"

"I think something has happened to him," Filip said, his expression grim. "Because that's the point, isn't it? Christoffer wouldn't do this. He wasn't depressed or bullied or angry. He was fine."

Zaria looked hopelessly at the group. "So we give up?" she asked, her voice high and thin. "We can't give up!"

"There's nothing more we can do," Aleks said. "Even if we wanted to help, what could we do? The adults have more resources."

Zaria shook her head, tears welling up in her violet eyes. "He's our friend."

"Come on, Zar-Zar, Geirr and I will walk you home," Filip said. He waved glumly to Aleks, who nodded.

Zaria went with the boys reluctantly. All three mulled over their thoughts, the silence thick. Nobody was willing to disturb it. As they crossed the scrollwork bridge, Zaria looked to the water. There were no swans tonight. The street noises of cars passing were faded in the distance. The quiet hum of insects drifted in the air.

"So the princess returns," a cold voice sneered, stopping Zaria in her tracks.

"Who the hell are you?" Filip demanded, edging himself in front of Zaria. He stood tall and square, feet planted firmly on the bridge, prepared to fight the creepy old man before him.

Olaf chuckled, hidden in the shadows. "You be her bodyguard, eh?" he said to Filip before turning his gaze to Zaria. "It's too late, Princess. You be breaking your promise, and I collected my fee."

"Wh-what?" Zaria asked, gripping the back of Filip's jacket.

"You'll not touch her," Filip stated coldly, clenching his fists. "Don't come any closer."

"Yeah," Geirr said, trying to look menacing in preppy clothes. "Don't come any closer or we'll fight you."

"Princess not be having manners and neither be her guards," Olaf said. He emerged from the shadows and laughed again, when Geirr's dark skin paled. Filip's face turned stony. "You be no match for me youngsters. I may be old, but don't be deceived. I be very, very strong."

Geirr looked at Zaria and Filip, before returning to Olaf. His blue eyes were nervously darting all over the creature in front of them. "What are you? Who are you?"

"He's Olaf, the river's guardian. He's a troll," Zaria answered, her heart hammering in her throat. "And he's real."

"A troll!" Geirr cried out, his big blue eyes widening in disbelief. "No way."

"He's not human," Filip replied. "Or homeless."

She looked over Filip's shoulder and glared at the troll. "Did you eat Christoffer?"

Olaf cracked a wide toothy grin, as if he'd been expecting that question. "Nothing you could do, Princess, if I did. But no, your loyal subject be safe for now. I know how much he means to you."

"What are you going to do to him?"

"Sell him to the highest bidder at the market. He will be enslaved and worked to death in the caves most likely. Very grueling work. Boy probably won't last long. They never do. You humans be so frail."

"You can't do that!" Zaria shouted, upset and trying to get around Filip. He held his arms out, blocking her path. Geirr grabbed her shoulder and held her in place.

"I can, and I will Princess –" Olaf said, "– unless you be getting me something."

"Yes, yes," Zaria said. "Enough food for you to feast on for a year."

"No!" Olaf shouted. "I not be wanting that. No. I want you to retrieve something for me."

"Steal?" Zaria squeaked, her bluster fading. "Steal what?"

Olaf's dark black eyes glowed faintly in the settling dusk. "The Hart of Gloomwood Forest."

"A heart? What heart? Where is Gloomwood Forest?" Geirr asked, biting his lower lip, crossing and uncrossing his arms.

"Gloomwood Forest is north. If you be following my river, you be reaching it. I be giving you five days. You must retrieve the Hart and bring it to my waters. If you do, I spare your friend and free him."

"And honor our first agreement," Zaria added, her lips pressed firmly together. She wasn't going to let Olaf trick her again.

"Why be I to honor it when you did not?"

"Because," Zaria said, crossing her arms, suddenly sure of one thing. "You never wanted to eat me or him in the first place. You always wanted this heart thing."

Olaf's eyes narrowed. "Clever, clever, clever Princess. Figured me out did you?"

"How far north?" Filip asked.

"Two days travel by river travel."

"I want your word," Zaria insisted, firmly. "We get you the heart. You let Christoffer go free. Honor our first agreement about crossing the river unharmed – for me and my friends. And… and…"

"And?" Olaf prompted.

"And you will provide us a boat," she finished, thrusting her chin out.

Olaf barked a laugh. "A boat?" He laughed some more and sobered when he noticed Zaria staring him down. "Fine, a boat and yes, I promise. My word be my honor, unlike you Princess. I be not breaking it."

"Good," she breathed. "Five days, Gloomwood Forest, the heart, and we're done with our dealings."

"Good luck, Princess," Olaf taunted, climbing to the top of the rails. "You be needing it."

And with that parting shot he slipped off the side. The boys ran over to get a look, but Zaria knew Olaf wouldn't be there or in the water. There had been no splash. Olaf had simply disappeared.

Chapter Three: Evading Parental Supervision

Geirr took out his mobile phone and quickly called Aleks to fill him in on this new development. While he was doing that, Filip watched Zaria.

"So, you met this troll before?" he asked, keeping his voice low. There was an edge to it.

Zaria nodded miserably. "Yes. I even told Christoffer and my parents about Olaf. Nobody believed me. And then I didn't believe myself. I thought perhaps I misremembered or – or dreamt it. After a while it didn't seem real."

"And when Christoffer went missing you didn't think of it then?" His eyebrows scrunched together in disapproval.

Zaria shook her head. "I should have. I'm so stupid. Why didn't I connect the dots sooner?"

Filip muttered an oath. "So what was this first deal you made with the troll?"

Zaria bit her lip. "He wanted to eat me and obviously that would be bad, so I convinced him not to eat me."

"Like in *Three Billy Goats Gruff*?" Geirr asked, stuffing his phone into his back pocket. He whistled. "That's gutsy. Don't you know anything about trolls?"

"Well, Scandinavian folklore says they're easily tricked due to pride –"

"Wrong!" Geirr cut-in. "According to Alek's gran's stories, they are very cunning. Trolls know exactly what to say to you to get what they want from you."

"How was I to know? All the books said differently."

"Do you always believe what you read?" Geirr asked. "This troll let you think you duped him, but instead you stepped neatly into his trap. We need to get a move on it. Let's go."

"Olaf," Zaria whispered as they finished crossing the bridge. "The troll's name is Olaf."

Geirr shook his head, looking over his shoulder to ensure they were well away from the water. "His name is not important right now. We need a plan to find Christoffer. We can't give the troll what it wants. If we do it'll be worse for us I'm sure."

Filip glared at Geirr. "How do you suggest we do that? The only way to rescue him is to retrieve the heart of Gloomwood Forest. I never heard of Gloomwood Forest. Our only direction to it is north of here. That's not very helpful."

"But we'll have a boat," Zaria said.

"And unless it's magical, we're going to have to navigate it by ourselves."

Zaria worried her lower lip. "I have old maps of Europe at my place. I got them for my last birthday."

"You got maps for your birthday?" Geirr said, laughing. "Your parents must not love you to get you maps."

"They're vintage, and I asked for them when we heard that dad would be transferring to Europe,"

Zaria said hotly, upset that Geirr would think her parents didn't love her. She knew they did. "They're hanging on my walls."

"Stop picking on her, Geirr," Filip said, quickening his pace. "Wasn't it you who said we needed to hurry? Let's get to Zaria's. She'll get her maps, stuff her backpack with clothes, food, and items for the next five days. We'll tell your mother that you're coming over for a sleepover."

"But it's Monday," Zaria said. "I don't think she'd go for it."

"Tell her school was awful and that we're all taking the day off tomorrow to get our heads on straight and maybe search again for Christoffer."

Zaria nodded and scurried up the stairs to her apartment. The boys followed and kept her parents busy. The Colonel didn't really approve of a mixed sleepover, but Merry was delighted to see the children embrace Zaria into their group. She also felt that it would do Zaria some good to avoid school for the next day or two. It was really too soon to be back around the probing stares of the other students. When Zaria came back down, jumping the stairs two at a time, the Colonel halted her with a hand on her shoulder. He stared down at the boys.

"I want the phone numbers for both of your parents," he said in his sternest voice and continued in a tone that brooked no discussion. "I will also drive you to the next house and take you to the last. I want to know it's approved by your parents and I want to know that they are paying attention. No funny business, do you understand me?"

"Papa," Zaria hissed. Her cheeks flushed with embarrassment.

Merry gave Zaria a hug and a kiss. "Call me if you change your mind for any reason, okay, sweetheart? It doesn't matter how late. Your father or I will pick you up." Zaria nodded, the red in her cheeks deepening. "Be careful driving tonight," she told her husband.

He nodded, slung Zaria's backpack over his shoulder and bussed his wife on the cheek, before escorting the children outside and down to the carport.

***

Geirr's parents didn't have a problem with him sleeping over and Filip had texted his mother to forewarn her of the planned sleepover. She was the most reluctant, but Filip knew how to charm his mother and by the time the three children arrived with the Colonel everything was approved, including an order for pizza to be delivered.

The Colonel clasped hands with Mrs. Storstrand and introduced himself, when she answered the door. The children not wanting to be a part of the conversation sneaked around them to Filip's room.

"Filip, dear," Mrs. Storstrand called out as they hurried down the hallway, "– your friend Aleks is already in your room. Go ahead and call for pizza, when you and your friends are hungry."

"Thanks, Mum!" he called back and shut the door quickly. He turned around and nodded to Aleks. "I think it's time to tell her."

"Tell me what?" Zaria asked, confused. She looked between the boys and saw them nod together.

Aleks drew in a deep breath and let it out gustily. He lifted his closed fists up and slowly revealed what was inside. Zaria didn't know what she was looking at – the object was shaped like an egg and shiny, but it had an odd hue which changed in the light between blue and purple. The whole surface of the object was perforated in several places with stars.

"It's a stargazer," Aleks said, holding it out for Zaria. As she examined it, he continued, "It's an object my grandmother gave me that day she discovered I was a changeling."

Zaria's head snapped up abruptly. "You're kidding me, right? You're a changeling? As in baby-swapping? As in fairy?"

Aleks nodded. "Yeah, and apparently Grams was one too, which she says is unusual. Fey rarely child-swap anymore, and if they did, it wouldn't be in the same family. That's why Grams gave me the stargazer. It's a –"

"So do you have special powers?" Zaria interrupted, her violet eyes bright and eager. "Can you fly? Do you have wings? You look so normal."

Aleks laughed. "Fey are not tiny woodland creatures. I can't fly. I don't have wings. My nose is slightly sharper and pointier though. And if Grams is right I will never grow facial hair. Being among my human families has softened the most distinguishable feature – pointed ears."

He lifted his hair off his ears. They were very slightly pointed and without the foreknowledge that Aleks was a changeling, wouldn't have registered as strange. Zaria touched the tip of her finger to the edge of his ear and traced her finger along the edge.

Aleks shivered and knocked her hand away. "Quit that."

"Sorry," Zaria murmured. "This is all so strange."

Aleks nodded. "When Geirr told me about the troll, I knew things were about to get wildly different and that we'd need the stargazer. Grams always said it was for adventures, I just never thought it would be for one like this."

Filip plucked it out of Zaria's hand and tossed it into the air, catching it on the downturn of the parabola. "So are you going to tell her about it or are you going to keep her in suspense?"

Aleks made a face. "I was getting to that, but she wanted to discuss magical powers, which by the way, I don't have. I can sense direction, and I'm great on camping trips."

"The whole commune with nature thing," Geirr added.

Aleks nodded. "But I also like video games and comic books and action movies. Normal. See?"

"Okay," Zaria agreed. "So what is the stargazer?"

Geirr snatched it out of Filip's hand, when he tossed it again. Geirr twirled it across his fingers with great agility. "Simply put, this little fella is going to get us out of parental supervision."

Zaria's brow furrowed. "How can it do that?"

"Practice run?" Geirr asked Aleks.

"Sure," Aleks replied.

Geirr tossed the stargazer at Zaria. "Listen close. Find the largest star and press your finger inside the hole until you hear a sharp click. NOT YET!" Geirr admonished. Zaria snatched her finger back and gazed meekly at Geirr. "When you've discovered what it does, you will want to press your finger into the smallest star. It's going to be hot, but do it anyway and click the button in the hole. Got it?"

"Press button in largest star to start whatever it is you want to show me and press the button in the smallest star to end it."

"That's right," Aleks said. He made a motion at her. "Go ahead. Have fun."

Zaria took a deep breath and gingerly put her finger into the largest star. Her finger brushed against the metal of the egg. It was cold, which made her jump. She'd been expecting heat. The boys watched her with bemused expressions, and Zaria firmed up her nerve. She pushed the button and heard the click.

Aleks, Filip, and Geirr continued to watch her. Zaria watched them back, not sure what she was supposed to see. At last she got annoyed and tossed the egg back to Geirr. "Nothing's happened," she complained.

The stargazer bounced off of Geirr's chest and hit the floor. Nobody moved. Zaria blinked. "No way," she breathed. She reached out to wave her hand in front of Filip's face.

He didn't blink. She clapped her hands in front of his nose. He didn't flinch. She poked him in the ribs. He didn't move.

"Ha!" Zaria laughed, delighted. This was an opportunity too good to miss.

She ran out into the hall, looking for Filip's parents. They were seated on the couch watching television, which was also paused mid-program. She checked their breathing. They were breathing, albeit slowly. She attempted to measure their pulses, but found it too difficult to follow the counts.

She flipped the channel to mess with them a little, ran back upstairs, found the master bath and grabbed Mrs. Storstrand's makeup kit. She ran back to Filip's room and quickly smeared blush and lipstick on all three boys, before rushing back to replace the kit. She didn't try to make it look pretty.

When Zaria was back in the room, she took one last moment to admire her handiwork. Just as she was about to press the button in the smallest star, she had a thought. Rummaging in her backpack, she grabbed her mobile and snapped a few pictures for posterity.

Then she replaced the phone, attempted to find the spot where she'd been standing earlier before pressing the first button, and reached into the smallest star.

It was very hot, just like Geirr had said. It wasn't quite painful, but it was warmer than she'd like. Zaria quickly pressed the button and snatched her finger back.

Filip was the first to start laughing as Geirr cursed and backhanded his face. Alek scrunched his nose in disgust and followed suit, but when it was over his eyes were twinkling.

"I would've worried about you, kid," he said, ruffling her hair, much to her annoyance, "– if you hadn't pulled a prank. Now let's order that pizza. Zaria, get out your maps."

***

Just after midnight the children gathered around Aleks and held hands. "Here goes nothing," he murmured and clicked the button.

Because they were all touching when the button was clicked, the children weren't frozen in place. They collected their gear and proceeded to the front door. Filip taped a note to the door for his parents, just in case the stargazer's effect wore off.

As Aleks explained, they had done this many times before to extend their weekends. Because really what kid wouldn't love to have a longer weekend? Zaria would have loved to have a stargazer too in order to read more books. There was never nearly enough time to read all the books on her to-be-read list.

This adventure would be different. Always before, they had stayed indoors. Now they would leave the house and Aleks didn't know if it would work. The longest they'd used the stargazer was forty-eight hours, but now they needed to use it for five days or more. Nobody knew for sure if it would hold or if the effect would transfer to the outside world, but it was their only option if they wanted to save Christoffer.

The first sign they saw that told them the stargazer was going to work, at least partly, was when they encountered a man walking his German shepherd. The man and dog were frozen in place, although the dog was growling faintly as if it knew something was happening. The children scooted away and hurried down the street. Their footfalls slapped the pavement and their backpacks jangled as they ran. It was no surprise that Aleks was in the lead.

Zaria was the least active of them and called for the boys to slow down. Filip and Geirr agreed and started walking. Aleks kept running in place, the extra weight of the tent not even slowing him down, until Geirr told him to knock it off. Then he too joined them at a much more reasonable pace. They reached the bridge, and by the bank, halfway hidden by the bridge was a wooden boat.

"Tricky, tricky, Princess," Olaf said, appearing beside the boat. "Just because you freeze the night, does not give you extra time. You will still have five days, whether the sun rises or not."

"So it'll hold?" Filip asked, pushing his blond hair off his face. "That's good news for us."

Olaf curled his lip in a sneer. "It'll hold humans, but not those with magic. They'll know and understand. You can't fool me."

Zaria stepped forward, hitching her backpack up higher as she went. "No trickery. We just needed to avoid adult supervision on our mission. Now that we're here, will you tell us more about the heart so we can get the right object for you?"

Olaf tilted his head to the side and stared at her curiously. "You not be knowing the Hart?"

Zaria shook her head.

Olaf cracked a wide and wicked smile. "Princess, you be wanting to seek out the Álfheim."

"The land of elves…" Zaria murmured, thinking hard. "They guard the river of the dead."

"You beasties best be going," Olaf said hastily, scratching his chest and frowning. "Or soon your time be up and your friend be lost."

"Right," Zaria said, walking the rest of the way forward and climbing onboard the boat. It wobbled beneath her as she took her place. "Come on guys, we got a heart to find."

Aleks climbed in next and tossed his backpacking gear into the nose of the boat under the seats. Geirr did the same with his, but Filip kept his on him and joined the party last, giving the boat a push to launch it into the river. Olaf stood on the bank and watched as Geirr started the motor, and they crept into the center of the river.

Aleks pointed which way to go, and they were off. When Zaria looked back, Olaf had disappeared. She shivered in the night breeze and hastily pulled out an extra scarf to tie around her neck. The adventure was about to begin… why again did she think this is what she wanted? Perhaps ordinary wasn't so bad after all.

Chapter Four:
The Peasouper Bellows

Zaria and Aleks consulted the largest map, and together found the best course to travel north. Aleks gave Geirr a compass he had packed, and Geirr secured it next to the rudder-handle. Filip passed around the thermoses of hot chocolate he'd put together, and they all sipped at them, grateful for the warmth.

Zaria watched the water, an idea weighing heavily on her mind. "If Christoffer knew Aleks is a changeling, why didn't he believe me about a troll?"

Filip's mouth pressed into a thin line. "I wish I knew. I'm sorry I was angry at you before. If you tried to warn him and your parents, and they didn't listen, what could you have done differently?" He shook his head, clenching his hands into fists repeatedly before forcibly letting his frustration go.

"I've been thinking about it," Zaria said quietly, staring at her thermos, watching the steam rise. "I wonder if I could have been more insistent. But I find it tough to be assertive." She bit her lip. "If I had been, things might have gone differently."

Aleks grabbed her hand. "Don't," he said. "It's no good to run yourself in circles like that. It's not like we were close friends and you could have told me or Geirr or Filip. You had no reason to do so. You didn't know about what I am."

"Exactly," Geirr said, nodding firmly, skirting the boat around a trio of frozen skippers. "The best thing to do now is move forward. Find this forest, locate the elves, rescue Christoffer, and get home."

"What do you know about elves?" Filip asked Zaria.

Zaria stared at them blankly. "I don't know. Probably nothing, considering I was wrong about trolls."

Geirr flushed. "Sorry, trolls are kind of my thing. I always loved Alek's gran's troll stories and had her repeat them over and over. Although having now met one, maybe trolls aren't my thing anymore."

Zaria shrugged. "I like fantasy. And I don't, you know, believe everything I read. Just because it's printed doesn't make it true. My mom taught me that. She's a college professor. She teaches online because of papa and the constant moving. Her favorite topic is yellow journalism."

"Cool," Aleks said, sipping his chocolate. "It's strange to see everyone frozen in place."

Zaria and Filip looked where Aleks was pointing. Groups of pedestrians up and down the river banks were stuck mid-step, mid-laugh, mid-life. It was bizarre, but it wasn't scary. Zaria felt better seeing them there than empty streets.

When they left the city behind and headed into open waters, Aleks pulled out a solar lantern and attached it to the bow. The lights of the city faded behind them until they winked out over the horizon. The dark stretched out before them, pressing in on the small lighted area thrown by the lantern. Geirr cautiously cranked up the engine and they flew across the water, navigating between the posts marking the channel.

Zaria's eyes adjusted to the dimmer light, and she was startled to see an owl swooping ahead of them, talons skimming the water. She pointed it out to the boys, and they all watched in silence as the creature flew into the tree line. Night sounds, previously absent in the city, started to reach their ears, as they traversed the waters. Did that mean that the stargazer's power stopped or never started out here?

Geirr switched seats with Filip and hunkered down to catch what sleep he could. Zaria felt the heaviness of sleep tug at her too, but she fought it, determined to stay awake as long as the others did. Aleks checked his backpack for supplies and spent time reorganizing their placement for better access.

Occasionally, Zaria took off her glove and trailed her fingers in the cold water, shaking the drops off before placing her hand back in the glove. The sharp sting of the frigid water woke her up. Slowly the landscape changed, and the children crossed through another town. And another. And another. Trees dotted the banks, but never thickened to imply that they were entering a true forest.

Eventually, Filip brought the boat to an idle and angled it toward another small town. It was the last Aleks saw on the map for several hundred kilometers.

It was just before dawn, and Zaria was exhausted. She nestled down to sleep, unable to keep awake with the boys any longer. Holding her gloved hands to her face to keep it warm, she was out instantly. The boys' conversation about where to find fuel drifted vaguely around her.

***

Zaria's stomach woke her hours later. She was starved, and the sunlight burned brightly behind her closed eyes. She was hot too. Feeling disoriented, she sat up and rubbed at her eyes and mouth.

"Never heard a girl snore so loud in my life," Filip teased, from the back of the boat. He steered it confidently and agilely through the fishing boats crowding the water way.

She blushed. "I do not snore," she mumbled.

Aleks laughed. "Just ignore him, he's making it up." He tossed her a plum. "Eat up. There's also breakfast bars, if you're still hungry."

"Have you slept at all?" she asked Aleks and Filip.

They both shook their heads. "I'm about ready to drop though," Filip admitted.

"Here," Aleks said, "let me take over. I'm still pretty fresh."

The boys resituated, and Filip grabbed a sweatshirt out of his bag and rolled it up into a makeshift pillow. Soon he was snoring like a banshee.

"The nerve," Zaria muttered, as she dug into her pack for a hair tie.

Aleks chuckled, and she threw him a wry glance. Then she gathered up her braids and pulled them into a ponytail. Cleaning up the plum juices with a handful of water Zaria felt like a new person, all the remaining vestiges of sleep gone.

Geirr woke not too long after that and chose a breakfast bar over the fresh fruit. "You'd think I'd be used to Filip snoring after all this time, but he can wake the dead." Aleks and Zaria laughed. "So where are we?" Geirr asked as he polished off the oatmeal bar.

"We're about to enter the main part of the fjords."

The river sank as the land soared higher and higher, until the children were but a speck shooting across the water. By now, Zaria was steering the boat and Aleks was sleeping. Geirr studied the map and used a pencil to edit the plotted course Aleks had marked. There was a shortcut he'd missed. It was a little off-shoot from the main fjord, but it cut across the land like a hypotenuse of a triangle. He showed it to Zaria and she agreed. When they came to it, Geirr helped her avoid rocks in the water and they navigated to the smaller river body.

Clouds gathered at midday, dark and lowering. The threat of snowfall worried the little group and they disembarked, pulling the boat up to the shoreline. Zaria and Geirr went to gather firewood, while Filip set up camp, and Aleks put together his portable fishing pole and cast into the river. He had a feeling about the water and thought he could snare a few fish.

Zaria rubbed her hands together and stomped her feet. "It's good to be standing and walking," she said to Geirr.

He nodded. "I don't know about you, but my legs were about to fall off from lack of motion."

Zaria laughed. "You win; it wasn't quite that bad for me. It's much better than an extended road trip."

Geirr stooped to pick up some decent-sized sticks, and Zaria bent to grab a few too. They talked amicably and walked, stretching their legs, until they were too burdened by their loads to keep going.

"My arms are going to collapse," Zaria huffed. Her breath fogged around her face, covering and then revealing a well-pinked nose and cheeks. "Let's head back to camp."

"Sounds good to me," Geirr said and turned around to do just that. Zaria followed and collided with him, dropping her load of kindling all over the ground.

"Hey!" she exclaimed, as she went to gather them. "Why did you stop?"

"I don't think we're going to find camp," Geirr said, worrying his lip. He juggled his armful of wood and pointed haphazardly forward. "It's like pea soup."

Zaria looked up from playing fifty-two pickup and saw what worried Geirr. In front of them was a wall of fog, thick, viscous, and impossible to see through. She gulped and carefully set down the pile she'd been working to gather again. Was it her imagination or did the fog seem to be breathing? It crept closer in stages. Not fast enough that she saw it while looking directly at it, but if she looked away and back, it most definitely moved.

"Uh, Geirr," Zaria said, slowly gaining her feet. "I think we should move and fast."

Geirr looked at her puzzled. "I don't think fast is an option here. Now if you pick up your stack and stick near me maybe we can *Marco Polo* our way back to the others."

"Geirr," Zaria hissed, her voice ratcheting higher. "The fog is moving." He didn't look impressed. The breathing sounds from within the fog grew louder, distressing Zaria. "No seriously, it's moving like it's alive."

Geirr looked back again and stared hard, trying to penetrate the fog with his gaze alone. Zaria started to ease away, firewood forgotten.

"Come on, Geirr, we have to move. Can't you hear the breathing?"

"That isn't you?" he asked, alarmed.

"No!" Zaria shouted. "Run!"

Geirr dropped his stack of firewood and ran, grabbing her arm as he whizzed past her. There was a deafening roar behind them. The duo panicked and put on more speed. Zaria ran, repeating the mantra in her head to not look back, to keep running, to not ever look back. She knew from books that the person who looked back was doomed. They would inevitably slow down and stumble in the process. It wasn't worth it. Whatever was crashing through the forest behind them wasn't worth it.

When another roar sounded behind them, Zaria jerked Geirr's arm. "Don't look back!" she warned.

But that didn't stop them from straining to hear what was chasing them, to try to locate it with their other senses. Their footfalls slapped loudly on the ground. Zaria was fiercely glad that it hadn't snowed. She did not relish trying to run through ankle- or knee-high thick snow. They would have been precariously slowed by its presence.

As it was, visibility was diminishing rapidly. Whispers of fog snaked around their ankles. Zaria got a stitch in her side and started wheezing. Geirr tried to drag her and then push her, but she was winded. He wasn't much better off than her, but desperation was clearly giving him the drive to keep forging ahead. Zaria was done. She had nothing left.

"I ca-can't keep going," Zaria gasped, falling into a limping run.

She held her side and struggled vainly to keep up with Geirr, but he quickly pulled ahead. Soon her fingers were slipping through his grasp, and they broke apart. The fog swirled like soup around her ankles. The breathing in its midst grew worse, if that were possible, all ragged and heavy. Shivers raced along Zaria's spine.

"Climb a tree!" Geirr yelled, racing to a thick trunk and quickly scrambling up it.

"Are you kidding me?" Zaria called back, limping the last few dozen feet to the same tree.

She looked up the length of it to discover Geirr halfway up. He was climbing it like a freaking monkey. Gamely, Zaria reached around the tree in a pantomime of a hug and searched for toeholds. She didn't get very far off the ground when she lost her footing and fell to the forest floor. And then it was too late. Their tormentor was upon them, and there wasn't anything Zaria could do.

A shadow appeared in the fog – large, menacing, and feral. It was as tall as a bear standing on two-feet and as wide as an elephant. It lumbered laboriously toward them, its deafening breathing straining the children's nerves with the rough rumbling sounds. Zaria pressed herself into the tree trunk, and squeezed her eyes shut.

Chapter Five: Fireside with the Stag Lord

The creature had intelligent pale gray eyes, the color of ice in shadow. Its face was shaped like a lion with two large fangs jutting out from its upper-lip. The body was heavily furred, the color reminiscent of a polar bear, but with black markings dotting its sides reminiscent of a snow leopard. The creature's arms and legs were covered in white opalescent scales, ending in giant bear feet (also scaly) with gleaming black talons. Thick, leathery, black-and-white wings sporting wicked talons attached at the middle of the back and folded in like an accordion by the front paws.

It was unlike anything Zaria had ever seen. She gazed at it in awe, her mouth hanging wide open. Her terror momentarily held at bay as she took in the glorious sight. Every breath it released sent billows of fog out around her. It reared again onto its back legs and pawed at the air, bellowing. Zaria flinched and ducked down, covering her head with her arms. She did not want to be its next meal. It would surely swallow her whole.

"It's wounded," Geirr said above her, his voice tense. "Something is sticking out of its back. There's blood."

Zaria peeked up around her arms, her braids dangling in her face. The creature had fallen back to four feet. Hesitantly, Zaria rose to a crouching position and made the daring decision to move toward the beast. It was the bravest thing she'd done her whole life.

"Zaria, what are you doing?" Geirr hissed. "Don't go near that thing!"

"Shut up, Geirr," Zaria said, creeping toward it.

With a shaky hand she reached for it. The beast stretched its neck, sniffing at her fingers. Zaria watched its face looking for signs of attack. The beast slumped to the forest floor with a gusty sigh. Fog billowed around Zaria's waist. She shivered.

"This is not a good idea," Geirr warned, watching as Zaria encircled the beast and finally saw the wound.

"Oh my," she whispered. "You poor creature. Who did this?"

With more gumption than she knew she had, Zaria grabbed the thick black spikes of its wings and hauled herself onto its back. The beast shifted in agitation and snarled. Zaria patted it on the shoulder.

"There, there," she soothed. "I'm going to take this –" Zaria looked at the object. "– spear, yes, spear, out of your back and you should be good as new."

The creature huffed and shrugged its shoulders. Zaria hoped that meant it understood her and steeling her nerve, she gripped the shaft and tugged hard. Zaria toppled end-over-end and fell to the forest floor as the beast roared in pain and jumped to its hind feet, clawing at the air. The spear fell beside her with a hollow clatter.

"ZARIA!" Geirr shouted, dropping from the tree. "ZARIA, ARE YOU OKAY?"

Zaria wanted to tell him she was fine, but the wind was knocked out of her. She was struggling to breathe and stay calm with the raging animal above her. It was flapping its wings and the wind from the movement cleared out the fog it breathed in a few short moments.

Geirr grabbed her by her armpits and hauled her back. They made it a few feet, when the beast quit yowling and landed heavily back to the ground. It turned to stare at them. Geirr swallowed thickly and looked a little faint. His dark skin paled under the steely stare of the beast. Zaria clutched at him, as she inhaled her first deep breath in the past few minutes. She wheezed heavily, her chest rising and falling with each gulp of air.

“Oh man,” Geirr moaned. “We’re toast.”

The beast snorted and used its wings to trap the children. And they were trapped. No way out. Geirr moaned again and Zaria used her returning strength to break his hold and stand beside him. She clapped him on the back.

“Breathe, Geirr,” Zaria said. “If the creature wanted to hurt us, we’d be dead already. Am I right?” This last was directed toward their captor.

Gray eyes watched closely and blinked. Zaria took that as an affirmative. She did a slow turn within the creature’s wings and marveled. “Geirr, isn’t he a beauty? Look at these gorgeous markings. There can be no more beautiful a sight in the whole world."

The creature rumbled. It reminded Zaria of a cat's purr, only louder and more gravelly, like boulders rubbing together. Geirr grabbed her hand and held it tightly, which was comforting for them both. Zaria reached out to touch one of the wings.

"It feels like a bat's wing," she said. "Or what I imagine one would feel like anyway. Soft and leathery, but thick, there's strength in these wings. You can see some of the veins where the sunlight hits him directly, although the fog obscures most of him. It must be a defense mechanism."

"Or offensive. It can hide in the weather of its own making and pounce on unsuspecting prey."

Zaria wandered closer, dragging a reluctant Geirr behind her. She reached its scaly legs and peered closer at them. They were really something. Opalescent, shimmery, white scales covered him from paw to shoulder. She touched him and felt the coolness of them. She ran her hand up and down marveling at the difference in texture depending on which way her hand went.

"This is so cool," Zaria told Geirr. "I wish I knew what it was. I've never heard of anything like him. You are unique, my friend."

"Is it purring?" Geirr asked nervously, looking over his shoulder at the lion-bear-beast. "Its head looks like a saber-tooth lion. Those fangs could tear us to ribbons. Claws too – look!"

"Don't fret," Zaria chided, moving to play with the thick fur of its collar and chest. "His fur is so warm compared to his scales. The fur and scales must both work together to regulate his temperature. He's like a big kitty."

"He's not a kitty. He's a mythical creature. He's neither cat, nor bear, nor snake, nor bird. He is dangerous. We need to go."

"I wonder if he's like a dragon," Zaria mused, ignoring Geirr. She was in nirvana, nerd-vana that is. "I wish I had a camera."

Zaria finished exploring the coarseness of the fur and turned her head up to meet its gaze. "Well Mister Kitty-Bear what do you plan to do with us now?"

It breathed fog for a moment, then scooped up both children in his claws and launched itself into the air. Zaria couldn't help it, she squealed. Geirr was too manly to squeal, but it certainly sounded like one to Zaria. The downdrafts from the wings were cold and mighty. The forest floor fell away, and they rose up and up into the air.

"Oh great," Geirr grumbled. "Just great. So we're not dinner now, but we can look forward to being the main course once we get to its lair."

"That would be worrisome," she concurred, but part of her thrilled to be in the air flying.

"I think I prefer flying lessons in a plane," Geirr said, looking a tad queasy. "The cockpit is really comforting you know. You don't feel like you're going to plummet to your doom in a plane."

"Just enjoy it!" Zaria encouraged. She was determined to take it all in – because this, she knew, was a once-in-a-lifetime experience.

Their winged companion covered a great distance in a short span of time. They were now high up in the mountains, and far below them ran the fjord looking more like a creek than a river. Zaria's teeth chattered wildly. Geirr's lips were blue.

"If-if he would just hold us by his chest, we'd be warm," Geirr said.

"H-he does-doesn't kn-know b-better," Zaria stammered.

Seconds later they were held in the warmth of the white fur on the creature's chest. Zaria buried her face into the fur and breathed in the musky scent. Her skin tingled where it warmed and her frozen nose thawed. The creature must have understood them.

Wind still whipped at them, tugging on their clothes, slapping against their cheeks, and seeking every possible inch of exposure between their clothes and their bodies. But it wasn't unpleasant. Their flying friend was toasty warm, and actually the longer Zaria was pressed there, the toastier she got. She was almost uncomfortable now and took pleasure in each nip of cold air.

"I shouldn't have spoken too soon," Geirr complained. "I'm starting to sweat. This guy's a furnace!"

Zaria laughed. "We are fickle are we not?" She pressed her ear against the creature's chest, enjoying the thumping sound of his heart and wings, as they worked in tandem.

Zaria's stomach dropped suddenly, and she looked about for the cause. They were descending rapidly, aiming toward a dark cavern in the cliff side. She hugged their friend closer and felt torn between exhilaration and terror, as they dove at a steep angle. Nervous laughter escaped her when their friend angled its wings like parachutes, jerking them up and back in a controlled stop. They landed lightly, much to Zaria's surprise.

The cavern was dimly lit, most of the light outside blocked by the snow-beast. A small fire smoldered in the back, casting stark shadows along the walls. Fog crept out from their position at the front of the cave, courtesy of their friend. An echoing rumble sawed through the air, setting Zaria's teeth on edge.

"Bones," Geirr whispered. "The shadows are reflections from bones."

Zaria looked again and gasped. Geirr was right. The shadows being thrown were bone-like. She glanced toward the fire looking for the source. They were not alone. A dark shape hunched in front of the fire had antlers. The antlers were huge – tall and wide with more points than Zaria could count.

"Did you bring them, Norwick?" the horned figured asked.

Norwick, as the beast was named, blew a deep sigh, sending out a wave of fog that reached their knees. He dropped the children to the ground, where they stumbled into each other, caught off-balance. When they righted themselves, Geirr moved forward briskly. Zaria followed.

"What is the meaning of this?" Geirr demanded, stopping at the man's side.

The man angled his head up, and Zaria realized he wasn't an antlered-creature, but wearing a white cloak made from animal hide with golden antlers attached to the hood. She looked the strange man over and noted his thick blond beard, grimy clothes, and skin which contrasted sharply next to the clean white pelt, and deep blue eyes.

"Sit, eat," the man ordered, gesturing to the fire, over which lay a trio of spitted rabbits. "I am Hector Woodworth, and you and your friends are in grave danger."

"Where are our friends?" Zaria asked, stepping around the man and the fire to sit opposite.

Geirr watched Hector with a frown, but after a moment, crossed over and sat beside her. "If you've hurt them, you'll regret it."

Hector chuckled. "They are not harmed, merely sleeping." He nodded over to the dark corner. "They are over there. Norwick frightened and exhausted them when he rounded them up."

"What are we in danger from? How did Norwick get hurt?" Zaria asked Hector as Geirr went over to the corner to see their friends.

The rumbling echoes which had become white noise ceased, and Zaria heard Filip curse. Zaria looked over, happy to see Filip, Aleks, and Geirr step back into the light of the fire. They looked like they had tumbled through mud and foliage. Aleks rubbed his eyes, plucking twigs from his hair and dropping them to the floor. Filip yawned loudly, scratched at some dried mud on his nose and took the seat beside Zaria.

"Good to see you, Zar-Zar," Filip said quietly, nudging her shoulder with his. "You look better than us, how come?"

"I don't know," Zaria said, gesturing to the mud. "Maybe I didn't fall into the river?"

Aleks took the other seat next to Zaria. "Didn't Norwick chase you too?"

"Yes," Geirr said, sitting between Aleks and Hector. "He did. I climbed a tree to get away from the ugly beast."

"He's not ugly," Zaria said. "He's gorgeous."

A cat-like yowl answered back.

"Norwick is a prideful beastie," Hector said affectionately. "He's saved my hide more than a time or two over the years."

"What type of creature is he?" Filip asked as he took one of the rabbits off the spit. He broke off some meat and handed it to Zaria before feeding himself.

"A winter-wyvern," Hector answered. "He's part reptile and part mammal. The species are skilled hunters, and prefer large game. They're also very playful. While they like to have fun, wyverns don't always know their own strength. So be careful. And, they're loyal to a fault, if you can earn their loyalty."

"Is a wyvern like a dragon?" Aleks asked, digging into another rabbit with Geirr.

Hector took a moment to reply. He ate a leg from the third rabbit and wiped his face with the back of his hand.

"Yes and no. Dragons are not beasts; they are shapeshifters. They use fire as a weapon and hate the cold. Norwick's fire is internal and meant to keep him warm, but since Norwick can breathe fire under duress, yes, he can be similar to a dragon. The smog from his breath is a smoke and fog mixture from the fire in his belly and temperature differences between his breath and the air."

"Wicked," Zaria said. She was all appreciation. "But why was he injured? Did something happen? Why are we in danger?"

"We were chased," Hector replied somberly, ripping another bite off the rabbit leg, "by a horde of trolls. This is troll country you're in now, and it's dangerous. They love to eat meat, and they don't care if the meat is elf, human, or deer. I'm surprised you were able to travel so far by river. There's a particularly nasty river-troll that guards it, and he doesn't like trespassers."

The boys all looked at Zaria. The rabbit meat was sawdust in her mouth. She swallowed thickly and started to cough. Hector handed her a metal flask, which she took gratefully and drank. Cool, refreshing water slid down her throat. She stopped coughing and ducked her head.

"I'm afraid it's all because of me," Zaria whispered.

Hector leaned forward, bracing his hands on his knees. "You gained passage on his river? How?"

Miserably, Zaria spilled the whole ordeal of how she met Olaf and the kidnapping of Christoffer. She didn't gloss over her idiocy in her dealings with the troll. But when she was about to reveal the object of their quest, the boys hushed her with a stern reprimand.

Hector eyed the group, and scratched his beard with the bone of the rabbit leg before tossing it over his shoulder. "All right, so you have secrets. I can live with that, everyone has a few. What's your final destination?"

Filip shook his head. "We can't tell you that either; it might give too much away."

Hector nodded. "My guess though is that you're heading north, which is also where I am headed. So I will give you this advice, stick near me for as long as you can. Norwick and I can protect you on this part of your journey. I'm a good hunter, so you will have food and not need to use your supplies until we part."

Geirr looked ready to argue, so Zaria cut him off. "Thank you," she said. "We accept. Can you tell us where you're headed?"

"Jötunheim," Hector answered, and then clarified when he saw her confused face. "Giant-land. I wish to trade with them for their beautiful home goods. They are known for their excellent craftsmanship and as a people with many great artisans among their ranks. They are also good farmers. You'd need to be if you're this far north."

"What do you trade them?" Aleks asked. "Clothes?"

Hector shook his head and took another piece of meat. He bit into it and gestured toward another corner of the cave. "Music."

"Music?" Aleks asked doubtfully.

"Music," Hector confirmed. "They love it, but can't play it – they say the instruments they make to their size don't carry the same resonance. And they hate the sound of their own voices, but love to hear singing. So I trade them music."

"How do you do that?" Filip asked as he gave Zaria the last piece of meat from their rabbit. "Trade them human-size instruments and sheet music?"

"You could," Hector agreed, "and they do appreciate them, but since they can't really play them without risking destruction of the instrument, I trade them in a more modern way."

"Digitally?" Zaria guessed.

Hector nodded. "They love iPads. It amazes them that humans could have placed so much music on such a tiny thing. Some of the giants still prefer vinyl records, but most love the diversity I can get them with iPads."

"So they listen to music on earbuds? How is that possible? Wouldn't they be too small?"

"Speakers," said Hector. "I also trade the giants speakers, batteries, chargers, generators, and other items to make the process work."

"Wow!" Zaria said. "Cool."

Geirr was skeptical. "And you can make a good living off of this?"

Hector laughed. "Elves and humans both love the giants' goods, not that humans know the items are giant-made. I tell them it's Scandinavian, which technically it is."

Filip took a drink from the water-flask and wiped his mouth before passing it to Aleks. Casually, he said, "And where do the elves live in comparison to the giants?"

Hector began to gather the remains of the meal. "They're about a three-day journey from the giants by horse. On Norwick it's about a half-day trip. Is that where you're headed – to Álfheim?"

Filip looked flummoxed. He sputtered a bit trying to figure out how to answer, when Aleks came to his rescue.

"We're just curious as to what you might trade with them. They probably don't need music. Everything I've heard about elves from my grams indicates they're wonderful musicians with crystal voices, like tinkling bells."

Hector rubbed his hands together and held them out to the fire. He said, "Elves trade in secrets and knowledge. They are very skilled in architecture and animal husbandry, particularly the exotic kind like Norwick here. I got him for a dozen secrets regarding human politics and six books on various sciences like solar energy, computer programming, and string theory."

"How do you get secrets?" Geirr asked, folding his arms. He tried to stare Hector down, but the man was oblivious.

"And that's my secret," Hector said with a wink at Zaria. She giggled.

"Seems kind of cheap," Filip said. "I mean you can pick up a lot of books for very little at a bookstore or online."

"True," Hector acknowledged. "Elves are curious that way, and I think it helped that Norwick didn't particularly like his previous owner. But now I think it is time everyone tries to get some more sleep before daybreak. We'll be moving slower, because Norwick is recovering from the troll attack. It'll be important to stay alert."

Zaria stood and tugged Filip's arm. He shuffled to his feet, stretched, yawned, and stretched again. "I'm ready," he said.

"Well, I need to go to the bathroom," Geirr grumbled. Aleks nudged him in the shoulder and waved him to follow. They went in the opposite direction.

Hector added a few logs to the fire, and then moved toward Norwick. He said, "It should be safe to sleep. Norwick and I will keep guard at the entrance."

"Good night, Hector," Zaria called out.

"Good night, Princess," he returned.

It was as she drifted off to sleep that Zaria wondered at his calling her that. She hadn't told him what Olaf called her and yet he used the same moniker. She'd have to remember to ask him about that in the morning.

Chapter Six:
When Trolls Ambuscade

Zaria understood what Hector meant about speed the next morning. Apparently winter-wyverns were not speedy on land. Get them airborne and their grace and agility became apparent, but on land it was another story. Compounding the group's troubles was the weather; it had snowed overnight.

From her perch on Norwick's back, Zaria scanned their surroundings at varying speeds according to

Hector's directions. She and Aleks, who sat behind her, were to watch for trolls. She kept her hand on the hunting knife Hector supplied her when they first started.

"Just in case," he had said, before handing another knife to Aleks.

Hector was well supplied, but he didn't have enough snowshoes for everyone, so he had directed Aleks and her to ride Norwick. He showed them how to saddle the wyvern properly and assisted them up onto Norwick's back.

As for other weaponry, he kept a rifle slung over his shoulder. To Filip he gave a fully stocked quiver and a large bow. Then he handed Geirr a fishing spear and the quintet and Norwick set off, heading north toward the giants.

"I can't see," Geirr complained to Filip, shuffling the spear to his other arm while batting uselessly at the smog drifting in front of his face.

Filip commiserated. "That's why Zaria and Aleks are lookouts. What I hate isn't Norwick's breath, but this snowdrift we're wading through. This sucks."

Zaria laughed. "I'm happy to switch any time."

"Not me," Aleks replied. "I like it up here."

Zaria laughed again and unzipped her jacket, warm despite the cold. Norwick threw off a lot of heat. She tugged off her gloves and stuffed them in her pockets as well. She gave a happy sigh as she wiggled her fingers in the cold air.

"Much better," she confided in Aleks, watching as he quickly followed suit.

"Oh yeah," he agreed. "Better."

"Do you two see anything?" Hector called from the front.

Aleks and Zaria spoke simultaneously. "No." "Nothing."

"Keep your eyes peeled," Hector warned. "Trolls are not likely to give up once they've found quarry in the area."

"We might have been safer on our own," Aleks whispered in Zaria's ear.

She frowned. "Why do you say that?"

"Well didn't Olaf give us safe passage?" he asked. "It seems to me we'd be better on water."

Zaria didn't like his conclusions. "Maybe, but what if these trolls wouldn't honor Olaf's deal?"

"We didn't see any trolls yesterday and were perfectly fine, until Hector sent his pet to ambush us."

Zaria stroked the fur on Norwick's neck. "I hear what you're saying, but Hector hasn't done anything to harm us. He's trying to help."

Aleks rubbed his freckled nose and shrugged. "I'm just saying, it's awfully suspicious that we ran into him before we ran into trouble."

"We won't run into trouble if we keep a lookout like we're supposed to do. You watch the right, and I'll watch the left."

***

As dusk fell on the group, it happened. From the shadows, a horde of trolls let loose a battle cry and charged through the smog. Many of them waved spears in the air, their snarling faces utterly terrifying.

"Circle up," Hector yelled, grabbing the back of Geirr's jacket and pushing him toward Norwick. "Stay close to Norwick. Don't let them get underneath him."

Geirr nodded, looking dazed as he flexed his shoulders and positioned his spear in front of him. Filip came up on his right and let an arrow fly. It flew into the mix and the trolls parted around it, flowing forward like water. Filip cursed and notched another arrow.

Anxiously, Zaria surveyed their attackers. She hadn't seen them coming. She failed her one duty. She gripped her knife, tensing for the right opportunity to slide off Norwick into the fray. Their attackers would reach the group soon, and then the real fight would begin.

The trolls blended into the background as quickly as they broke into the foreground, covered as they were in dirty white fur coats and tan breeches. They were not as lanky as Olaf had been – some were considerably bulky. Their skin was grayer, and she wasn't sure, but it looked like they had tails. Big droopy noses dominated their faces as they roared, covering the remaining distance in seconds.

"On your left!" Aleks called out. All three on the ground looked left and saw a massive troll lumbering forward from the tree line.

Hector raised his shotgun and fired at the enormous troll. The shells struck, but barely slowed the creature down. "He's their leader. If we can kill him, we might stand a chance."

"What are their hides made out of, steel?" Filip groused, shooting another arrow and watching it as it was deflected easily. He ducked the return fire.

Spears and arrows peppered the group, as Norwick bellowed and reared on his hind legs. Zaria squeaked. Norwick flailed, using his impressive size, and wings, and teeth to snap at the trolls. It was like riding a bucking bronco, Zaria thought. Jumping off Norwick into the fray was the last thing on Zaria's mind, as she struggled to hang on.

Something heavy collided with her, knocking her senseless. Zaria heard Aleks swear. He stabbed wildly at the troll who landed on them, but the thick shaggy fur on the troll's coat kept the blade from reaching flesh. Zaria was pinned under the troll's weight, his ghoulish breath making her grimace. She tried kicking her feet, but had little room in which to move.

"Stop struggling, cheeky girl," the troll growled. "We don't want to harm you."

"Get off her," Aleks yelled, shoving the troll. The two grunted and rolled, briefly crushing Zaria. She felt the air go out of her.

She gasped and struggled into a sitting position, searching frantically for the knife, but the weapon had been lost in the fray. So she did the first thing that came to mind, she pulled harshly on the troll's tail and kept pulling.

"Leave him alone!" she shrieked in its ear.

He roared and knocked Aleks off Norwick in a brutal blow to the head. Rounding on Zaria, he grabbed her by the wrist and bent it back. Zaria cried in pain and released her grip on his tail.

The troll pushed her into a sitting position and grabbed both her wrists. She tried to struggle but was quickly subdued with bindings. Then when she was unable to break free, he jerked her roughly and leapt from the back of Norwick. They tumbled in the snow.

"No!" Zaria cried. "Let me go! Let me go!" She tried to stand, but he knocked her legs out from under her.

"Kafirr wants to meet you, especially your friend. You best be going quietly," the troll growled. "No more fuss from you."

A sharp short jarring noise disturbed the night. The echoes of it, Zaria felt in her bones, even as the sound of Hector's grunt of pain reached her. She saw two trolls wrestle the rifle out of his grip and knock him out with the butt of it. Everywhere she looked, her friends were subdued, with limbs bound hand and foot.

"No! Stop!" she begged. Her captor laughed.

"You be issuing orders, little princess? Mangus don't know you to be following your commands."

Norwick was still rampaging, but his efforts were ignored as a team of trolls circled him with sharp multipronged spears. Every time he opened his mouth, Zaria saw deep red glowing brighter at the back of his throat. Was he building up for a fireball? She bit her lip, anticipating it, hoping for it.

"You think the beast will shoot fire, don't you?" Mangus asked, shaking her with his foot. "Us trolls know how to handle winter-wyverns."

And it appeared he was right. When the flaring red-orange glow in Norwick's throat grew bright one of the trolls threw something into his mouth. An explosion boomed violently, scaring Zaria. A pathetic whimper from Norwick alerted her as he curled instantly in on himself. Fog billowed from his nose, ears, and mouth in plumes.

"Dry ice grenade," Mangus said smugly. "It sublimes quickly in a winter-wyvern's belly. It's most unpleasant for them. Instantly squelches the fire, you see, and can leave the belly frostbitten."

"That's horrible!" Zaria said, aghast. "You're monsters."

The troll's face darkened with anger. "Shut your mouth, or I be shutting it for you."

Before she could respond the large troll leader entered into the midst of the group. "Good job, trolden, let's get home. Finish securing the beast. Bring them all."

Zaria's troll captor jerked her to her feet and pushed her forward, keeping a hand on the back of her neck the whole time. She and her friends were frog-marched to the tree line. Zaria watched in amazement when a group of them roughly pulled a tree out of the ground, the snow on its branches falling over them all. Under the tree was a large dark hole and it was here that Zaria stepped into the underground kingdom of the trolls.

***

The trolls sang boisterously in a garbled mix of languages about the glory of Trolgar, their kingdom. They were pleased with their successful ambush and were boasting of their prowess and vitality. Mangus was replaced by another troll as they marched.

Firelight from torches danced across earthen walls, as the group moved forward down endless dark passages. There were times when the corridor branched off and times when they took turns. Zaria attempted to memorize the pattern but after a while was befuddled by it all. She could only hope the others were able to keep it straight. If only Hector were awake. He would know what to do.

The further they went, the brighter the corridor became, lightening first by degrees and then so much the torches became unnecessary. Zaria was in the back of the group, her friends interspersed throughout the horde of trolls. She figured this was to keep her and the boys from talking and hatching escape plans. She craned her neck to see what was happening, but couldn't see over the shoulders of the trolls.

Loud rumbling sounds met the party, growing louder until in the crescendo of it, Zaria realized they were drums beating out a victory ballad. The earthen hallway expanded abruptly into a wide cavern, as tall as it was wide. They were at the top and the view below stopped Zaria in her tracks, until a rough hand shoved her forward.

Zaria craned her neck, looked in every direction, and couldn't believe what she saw. The cave was floor to ceiling covered in buildings, outcroppings, glowing windows, homes, businesses, and trolls. Trolls in colorful clothing bustled everywhere, lining the streets, waving at the troop, catcalling, cheering, hooting, and stamping their feet in a wild display of enthusiasm.

Zaria and her friends were marched through the main street, as wide as any human thoroughfare. She saw reindeer and wolves, here, there, harnessed, leashed, or roaming free. They reminded her of pets – horses and dogs – at least until a wolf snarled at her and snapped its jaws. She jumped away in fright.

The street ended at the foot of a large palatial structure. It soared all the way to the ceiling. Zaria couldn't determine if it was a fortress, castle, or palace. It sort of appeared to be all three with different architecture used all the way through it. Towers ascended in spiny, spindly, and spirally forms. The outer wall was deep, thick, and rough with archways staggered every now and then as an opening into an inner courtyard she couldn't quite see.

Soldiers lined the largest of the archways, spears, bows, axes, and swords stowed in gleaming perfection on their belts. Zaria gulped. Their stoic faces after the sea of cheerful citizens was terrifying. The troll leader of their group was greeted by the head soldier, who looked quite fetching in his uniform.

"Jorkden," the soldier troll greeted. "It looks like your team caught quite a delicious bunch of morsels."

Jorkden sneered. "Don't antagonize them, Morvin. I am to take them to see Kafirr."

Morvin curled his lip, stroking his mustache. "Of course they must see the king. Stow the weapons, and you can enter the palace."

It was clear to Zaria that Jorkden was reluctant to do this, but he made a motion to his trolden and they handed their weaponry over to the soldiers.

Zaria's shoulder was gripped harshly, and she winced. The hand did not shove her as expected. Cautiously she peered over her shoulder and saw Hector staring at her. He was slung like a sack of potatoes over a beefy troll. He looked small without his white stag cloak, and Hector was not a small man.

Run, he mouthed.

She shook her head. She wasn't prepared to run. Not yet. Not without her friends. Not without Hector and Norwick. She looked around; Norwick was trussed up on a large pole carried by many trolls. He looked so sad, her heart broke for the beast. She was going to free him, all of them, if she could. But how? In an underground kingdom surrounded by enemies how did one escape?

Hector frowned at her and mouthed, *Run*, again. She shook her head again. She couldn't rescue Christoffer on her own, although, someone really needed to rescue them first or Christoffer was going to be in for a worse fate. They would be too. Who knew what Kafirr wanted with them?

Jorkden led the party into the palace courtyard and stopped. The courtyard was a steamy place with plants and rocks and bubbling water from an engineered waterfall. It was beautiful and completely unexpected. Up at the top of a steep set of stairs stood a throne and on the throne sat a troll even bigger than Jorkden.

Zaria and her friends were forced to their knees as Jorkden took a stiff bow. "My king," he said, "I bring you fresh meat."

Chapter Seven: Inside Trolgar

The troll king, Kafirr, was as still as stone and the color of it too. His blue eyes were washed-out, but the intelligence and ferocity in them unmistakable. He wore a crown of frost. It glittered and glistened in the lights thrown from the sconces. His nose was sharp like a knife and dipped down to his upper lip. His hair was black, his teeth similarly colored, and his hands looked like claws. Zaria trembled under his penetrating gaze.

"Is that the Stag Lord?" the king asked after several long minutes of silence. His voice was rough and guttural, as if he'd been a chain-smoker for many years.

Jorkden nodded. "He is. My trolden and I captured him, his human companions, and his winter-wyvern. The wyvern is being taken to the training center, but if my king wishes to inspect the beast, I can have him brought here."

Kafirr's face remained stoic and expressionless. He gave Zaria the creeps. "And in their possessions? Did they have them?"

Jorkden motioned for one of trolden to step forward. The troll that did struggled under the burden of carrying the children's bags and Hector's equipment. He dumped it all the first chance he got. Two more trolls stepped out of the lineup and poured out the contents of the bags.

Everything was tossed helter-skelter. Zaria blushed, when her unmentionables appeared. Every embarrassing shade of pink, purple, and canary yellow fell out for all to see. Lucky for her, the trolls were ignoring her underwear for they had just unrolled the maps and were talking excitedly. Then the stargazer fell out of Aleks' backpack and was absently picked up by one troll who examined it.

"This item is hot," he said.

"Let me see," commanded Jorkden who snatched it and peered into the holes. "Magical. Perhaps from the witch in the woods?"

He looked to Zaria and the others to confirm, but nobody spoke. He smiled and tucked it into his pocket.

Aleks bristled. "That's mine," he growled. "My grandmother gave it to me."

"I think you mean, it's mine," Jorkden replied smoothly, oozing false charm. Then his mood changed like quicksilver, and he barked at the three trolden still rummaging through the children' things. "Thorkel, did you find them?"

"They're not here, sir," the troll on the right, who must be Thorkel, said. He wiped at his bulbous nose sullenly and elaborated, "We've searched. They don't have it."

The king was unimpressed. "Jorkden, this is the third time you've returned without the shoes."

"Your highness," Jorkden pleaded. "We captured the Stag Lord. He had Helena's shoes last –"

"Shoes?" Geirr burst out, confounded. "This is about some girl's shoes? Are you kidding me?"

Mangus who'd been standing nearby, stomped on Geirr's foot. Geirr yelped and glared at Mangus.

"Stuff it," snarled the troll.

Zaria looked to Hector. The man looked like he hadn't a care in the world. When Jorkden picked him up by the scruff and slammed him to the ground, Hector had the audacity to laugh. Laugh! Zaria couldn't believe it.

"Where are the shoes?" Jorkden roared, slamming a fist into Hector's jaw.

"He's going to get us killed," Aleks muttered, sending Zaria an I-told-ya-so look. "The trolls weren't after us. They were after him."

Filip stepped on Aleks' foot. Aleks flinched and glared at Filip. Filip raised a brow. "Would you shut it? Now is not the time for blaming anybody, not even Hector."

Zaria could have kissed Filip. "Exactly," she concurred, sticking her tongue out at Aleks. When Filip glared at her, she ducked her head.

"Back me up," Filip muttered before straightening and stepping boldly forward. "Excuse me."

The king's attentions were fixed on Jorkden and Hector's grappling. When he didn't turn to Filip, her friend lost some of his bluster.

"Ahem. Excuse me," Filip tried again.

This time the king looked at him, tapping his clawed nails on the armrest of his throne. The king arched a supercilious brow. Filip gulped. He looked like he wanted to shrink from the king's attention. Zaria nudged him forward, silently giving her support.

Filip took a deep breath, gathering his courage. He spoke in a rush. "We were with Hector last night. We know where he might have hidden the shoes."

Zaria wanted to kick Filip. This was his plan? "Filip, no!" she hissed.

Aleks piped up. "He had his wyvern collect us and took us to a cave. We can show your men the –"

"Trolden," King Kafirr interrupted.

"Huh?" Aleks asked.

"Trolls are not men. We're not puny humans. We're trolden, Changeling."

Aleks stammered, shaken that the king recognized him for what he was. "H-how d-did–"

"You smell like something disowned," the king supplied, before dismissing him with a flip of his wrist. "Now, Jorkden, take these fine human children and lock them in the dungeons. Then put Hector in the interrogation chamber. We're going to learn about this cave he slept in last night. Queen Helena's shoes will be ours."

***

"How could you?" Zaria demanded. Violet eyes burned into green. They were locked in the dungeon, deep in the bowels of Trolgar, where the earth was damp and dank.

"I just thought we could negotiate our release," Filip mumbled, his cheeks staining red from a mixture of indignation and embarrassment.

Aleks gave Filip a slap of comradery on the back. "Leave him alone," Aleks told Zaria. "At least he had a plan. It didn't work, but it's better than what the rest of us did."

"But he betrayed Hector!"

"So?" asked Geirr. "We're not friends with Hector. We met him last night. We have three nights left to rescue Christoffer and Hector is no longer a help to us."

"I can't believe you guys," Zaria muttered, clutching at her braids in agitation. "Hector wouldn't have been caught if he was riding Norwick. He went on foot because of us. He's now captured because he was trying to help us."

"By first putting us in danger!" Aleks retorted belligerently, his face reddening in anger.

Geirr laid a hand against Aleks, restraining him. "Look, we shouldn't fight about this. What is done is done," he said reasonably. "We can't help Hector or Christoffer if we are locked in this cell. We should be figuring out how to get out of here."

Zaria and Aleks lapsed into silent fuming, both grudgingly admitting that Geirr was correct, but equally unwilling to admit it aloud. Zaria kicked at a rock on the ground, scuffing her shoe in the dirt. The boys began examining the walls, the cell door, the ceiling, and the floor. The cell lacked furnishings and had no chains or metal rings in the walls. It appeared to be a hard-packed earth floor with stone walls.

Zaria pouted a minute longer before gritting her teeth and joining them. She knew they'd done Hector a disservice, but she also knew it wouldn't be corrected from in here. She couldn't help but think that they had none of their belongings, no weapons to help escape, and no food.

Zaria heard one of the boys' stomachs growl. An answering echo sounded in hers. She was hungry; they'd marched quite a bit today and tonight. But if the boys wouldn't complain, neither would she.

"We need to get the stargazer back," Aleks said after a while, when everyone had given up and settled to the ground. His head lulled against the stone surface of the wall behind him. "If we don't have it, we won't be able to undo the trick on Filip's parents and the city. Everyone will be frozen permanently."

"Our tasks keep piling up," Filip said glumly. "And none of it is easy."

Geirr scoffed. "Easy? There was nothing easy about this from the beginning." His stomach gurgled loudly. All the children could commiserate. "I'd kill for something to eat," Geirr muttered, taking a piece of stone from the floor and tossing it at the door.

It clanged loudly, the noise reverberating in the small space. There was no answer from outside. It appeared they'd been cheerfully neglected. Zaria knew why – they weren't a threat, nor could they escape. It was hopeless.

The night was slipping by faster than a landscape slid by a speeding train. Sleep was probably for the best. She closed her eyes and hunkered down, burrowing her face in the neck of her jacket for warmth.

Completely exhausted she slipped into slumber, and the boys soon followed suit.

***

"Wakey, wakey," a nasally voice said from the other side of the door. "Breakfast."

Zaria and the boys jumped to their feet and raced to the door. Through the window opening appeared hunks of meat on a bone. The children eagerly grabbed one each. Geirr took a vicious bite, sheering a large hunk of meat off in one gulp.

The troll cackled. "Healthy appetites, good. Water next."

He handed a few tumblers over. Zaria drank greedily from hers, slopping some down the side of her chin. The others were equally eager to slake their thirst.

"You have to let us out," Geirr said to the troll, wiping his mouth with his sleeve. "We are on a mission for Olaf, the river-troll."

The troll on the other side stilled abruptly. "Olaf of Glomma?"

Zaria nodded. "The very same. We're meant to retrieve something for him."

"I will tell the king." Then the window pass-through slammed shut.

"This is actually good," Aleks said through a mouthful of the mystery meat. "I wonder what it is?"

"Best not to know, man," Filip replied, ripping another chunk of meat off his leg bone and slurping it down. "That was inspired, Geirr. Brilliant even."

Geirr shrugged modestly. "It couldn't hurt. And it's not anything Hector doesn't already know, so if the king wishes to confirm it, he can ask the guy."

They continued eating in silence. Every bone was gnawed on, and all flesh stripped clean off. Zaria finished her water with a gusty sigh. "I'm full," she said.

Filip and Geirr concurred, with Geirr rubbing his belly. Aleks was frowning into his cup, but otherwise said nothing. Zaria thought he was probably still hungry. She should have saved him some of her food. She felt bad that she hadn't thought of it.

As time passed, Zaria began using her bone to draw in the dirt. She tried to draw Norwick, but couldn't get him to look right. She kept wiping him away and trying again. The floor soon became uneven, which just irritated her more. She moved over a bit to try again when her thought was arrested.

"Hey guys," she whispered, breathless with the idea.

"Yeah?" Filip asked. He was tossing his bone between one hand and the other.

"I have an idea," she said, her insides bubbly with excitement. "I know how we can escape."

All three boys looked at her with interest. "So, what is it?" Geirr demanded.

"We dig our way out." A bright smile lit her face as Zaria pointed at the depression she had made trying to draw Norwick and then pointed to the bottom of the metal door. "The floor is dirt. The door just sits on it and our troll friend just gave us tools." She pointed to the bones and cups. "We can dig a hole just big enough to escape and be out of here in no time!"

Geirr got excited. "It could work!"

"Brilliant, Zar-Zar," Filip said, giving her a fist bump.

Aleks hesitated. "But our 'troll friend' as you put it, is on the way to the king and will soon be back."

"So?" Geirr asked. "It can't take that long to dig a hole and really, we don't even know if the king will care. Who says river-trolls and cave-trolls get along at all?"

Filip shrugged. "I'm in. Let's get to work."

The four of them gathered around the base of the door. They each tried a few things to get the dirt loose. Filip found that the quickest way was to stab the dirt several times with the sharpest end of the bone. The bone broke through the hard surface just enough to scoop some of the dirt into a tumbler.

At first the pace was slow where each bit of dirt removed was a coordinated effort. But soon they could abandon the bones and use their hands and the tumblers as shovels to scrape the dirt away. The depression was growing, but they needed to move it out under the door and up.

They worked together. Each one methodically scraping, scratching, and scrapping the dirt until at last a small hole appeared letting the outside light shine down. Filip and Zaria let out exclamations of triumph. Eager fingers grappled against each other as the children hurried to widen the hole.

As they dug the hole out, it took longer to remove the excess dirt away, for they brought the dirt from one side of their hole to the other. But soon, soon, they were able to stick an arm through and not long after that had created a space beneath the door in which one of them could escape.

Zaria was the natural choice, because she was the smallest. She crawled under, contorting her body and bracing with her feet to pull and push her way through. Her shoulders scraped unpleasantly against the underside of the metal door. Hands pushed at her backside and with a *pop* she was free.

"What do you see?" Aleks asked.

Zaria looked around and saw winding corridors in both directions. There only appeared to be a few other doors on their stretch of the hallway. Nobody was about. "Coast is clear. Come on!"

Next to make his way through the hole was Geirr. He was closest in size to Zaria. When he got his arm and head through the hole, Zaria leapt forward to help him. She grabbed his elbow and tugged.

"Ow!" Geirr grumbled, "Watch it!"

"Don't be a baby," Zaria shot back and tugged some more.

Geirr struggled a bit, but it was clear he was being assisted on the other side of the door as well, and he too was free. The hole did not make it through the boy's struggle intact. It was now partially collapsed.

"Oh no," Zaria groaned.

She and Geirr got down on their hands and knees and quickly scooped the dirt out. Aleks and Filip worked from the other side. When Zaria's fingers met Aleks' she let out a small sigh of relief.

"You next, Filip," she told the boys. "Then Aleks."

With the hole wider, Filip was able to wriggle through it a little better than Geirr. He was still mightily clumsy as he labored. Aleks had to tell him twice to stop kicking and let himself be pushed.

Luckily for them all, the hole did not collapse a second time. Unlike the others, Aleks came through on his back, using his feet to propel himself up and out. Filip and Geirr grabbed his hands and yanked him hard. When Aleks came loose, the boys all collapsed on the floor in a heap.

"That was unpleasant," Aleks murmured when he caught his breath. "Let's not have to do that again. I feel filthy."

"Look it too, mate," Filip rejoined.

They were all grinning at each other. Aleks was right; they were filthy, covered in dirt from head to toe. They were especially grimy under their fingernails. But damn, if it wasn't good to be out of the prison cell.

"So now the question is," Zaria began, "how do we get out?"

Filip and Geirr looked at Aleks with expectation. Zaria wondered at that for a moment before she remembered Aleks boasting of his sense of direction. She looked to him hopefully.

"You know the way?" she asked.

Aleks shrugged. "Maybe. I have a good idea. It's what I usually go on, and it hasn't failed me yet."

"Lead on," Filip encouraged.

Aleks pointed to the left and started loping that way. The others followed. It was a good thing Aleks was prepared to lead them, because each hallway they turned down looked like the next and Zaria was hopelessly lost. Nothing and everything looked familiar. She couldn't make out any landmarks to give her a place of reference. But Aleks was confident, and for now that was all that mattered.

Chapter Eight: The Frozen Subterranean River

It turned out that Aleks did know where they were. He led them through the endless series of identical passageways and out into the shadows of the palace courtyard. They spied a few trolls bustling about doing early morning chores. Here they halted, breathless, jubilant, and anxious, knowing at any moment they could be spotted.

"Halfway out of here," Geirr said with a smile. "You did it, Aleks."

"Yeah, way to go, man," Filip added, clapping Aleks on the back. "We could not have done it without you."

"That was amazing," Zaria agreed, tucking her braids behind her ears. "You were amazing. I was totally confused. Everything looked the same to me."

Aleks shrugged and modestly waved away their praise. "It's as natural to me as breathing. No big deal."

"Easy for you to say," Geirr joked. "Not so for the rest of us mere humans."

Aleks gave Geirr a dirty look.

Filip said, "So what do you say? Let's get out of here for good."

Zaria frowned. "What about Hector? Norwick?"

"And my stargazer?" Aleks added.

Geirr thought for a moment. "It would be better to leave now before anyone notices we are gone, and we can always return for the stargazer." Zaria coughed. "And Hector and Norwick," Geirr added, placating her. "But only after we retrieve the heart of Gloomwood Forest and give it to Olaf. Then we can have all the time we need."

Just then, a troop of trolls rushed into the courtyard from all directions. The children drew back and pressed themselves against the stone wall, holding their breath lest they be seen. Morvin appeared in the palace doorway, glaring down at the scene. He stalked over to the assembled group and held a wicked looking spear high over his head. The noisome trolden silenced abruptly at the signal. The children watched, holding their breath. Had their absence been discovered?

"The Stag Lord has escaped," Morvin thundered, his mustache bristling. "But he will not get far!"

The trolden roared their approval, beating their fists on their breastplates. The children looked at each other astonished. Hector had also escaped? How?

"We will hunt him down and strip him of his antlers and feast on his bones. Search everywhere. Do not let him get away. Check the dungeons; he might try to rescue the human children. And make damn sure that his beast is secure. Go!"

The troop dispersed rapidly, the sounds of many feet and clanking weapons and armor echoed all around the courtyard. Morvin slammed his spear on the ground and watched his trolden hurry to do his bidding. The children watched him from the relative safety of their hiding space in the shadows.

Morvin seemed content to survey everyone running to and fro across the courtyard. He was less pleased when Jorkden appeared beside him. It was clear the two trolls did not get along. Jorkden started gesturing and saying something. Morvin's face grew darker with each gesticulation Jorkden made, until the two erupted, trading punches.

Aleks put a finger to his lips, and edged along the wall, careful to keep behind the engineered waterfall and foliage. Filip went next and Zaria followed. Geirr took rearguard. Every one watched the grappling trolls, hoping they were too enamored of their fisticuffs to look about them.

It was with a sigh of relief that the children slipped out of the palace courtyard and into the wide thoroughfare of the city. Like thieves, they slinked into the shadows and hurried for the protection offered by nearby buildings. City noise murmured around them, regularly gaining and dropping in pitch.

This morning, Zaria saw that the light in the city reflected off thousands of mirrors hung at the top of the cavern. It hurt to look at the ceiling where the light bounced around the most. She wondered what had lit the city in the night. Perhaps fire. It made sense to her that it could be fire.

As soon as he was able, Aleks took a path that led away from the main street and into the alleyways. The buildings towered like stalagmites, each one forcefully jutting toward the ceilings. Minerals and water even dripped steadily down the buildings so that they glistened in the light.

It looked all so normal in some respects. Laundry hung on lines strung behind buildings, pots of flowers and ferns decorated balconies, smells of breakfast cooking wafted tantalizingly down from above, and voices rose and fell from open windows as conversations took place around kitchen tables.

Then in other ways it would be clear that this wasn't a human city. The buildings were obviously strange primitive dwellings hewn from rock. Wolves with their glowing eyes tracked them from the dark alleyways where light hadn't yet filtered. Geirr stepped in reindeer poop, making many *errgh* sounds much to Filip's amusement.

A horn sounded from the direction of the palace. Trolls raced out to their balconies in various stages of dress. The children lurched across a street into a gloomy alleyway and tried to make themselves small. Shouts echoed in the underground cavern as the trolls yelled at each other to figure out what was going on.

Aleks and Filip ducked their heads around the corner to watch the happenings. Filip laid a protective hand on Zaria's shoulder. He gave her a lopsided smile before peering around the corner again. They all held still, holding their breath, waiting for whatever happened next.

Another horn blasted and the streets exploded with war cries. The happy cheerful citizens of yesterday vanished in an instant, replaced by animal fury. It frightened Zaria, and her whole body trembled. When Aleks and Filip ducked back into the alleyway, their faces were grim.

"They know we've flown the coop," Filip said.

"And something about a Wild Hunt…" Aleks muttered.

Zaria gasped. "No!"

The boys looked at her in alarm. "What is the Wild Hunt?" Geirr asked.

Zaria worried her lip, unsure how to explain. "Well, from stories it's the most terrible hunt of all. The hunters fly above the ground and hunt from above by magic. If you're human and you witness the hunt you die... or you're dragged into the underworld, which might be the same thing."

Geirr laughed. "Considering these trolls are probably in the mood to kill us, I guess it doesn't matter, does it?"

She gave him a cross look. "I'm serious. The Wild Hunt is bad news. I've never heard of trolls running one though." Zaria frowned at them. "In all my stories it has been fairies, spirits of the dead, or Norse gods running the hunt. Never trolls."

"So what kind of cavalcade are we expecting?" Aleks asked.

"Probably reindeer, wolves, and angry trolls," Zaria said. "I haven't seen any other animals down here, have you?"

Filip shook his head. "So we have to avoid flying reindeer? Excellent. We're being hunted by a very ugly Santa Claus and his uglier minions."

Laughter erupted from Aleks. "I hope we're on the nice list."

Filip grinned back. "I don't think our chances are good for that. If Santa and his helpers are hunting us down, I think it means we're solidly on the naughty list."

"You two are ridiculous," Zaria said, laughing nervously. "But seriously, we need to get going."

Echoing howls punctuated her declaration which sprung the children into action. Aleks took point again, and the others followed his lead blindly. They kept close and nobody was ever out of reach. Everyone was on alert, looking for trouble.

Zaria didn't espy any wolves now as they ran. The wolves knowing eyes were trained elsewhere as the trolls worked to track them down. But it was only a matter of time. She feared they were to be hunted by a whole pack of wolves.

They ran for several minutes, winding their way through the city. Whenever the noise from the hunt became more acute, Aleks would change directions and put on speed. They had so far avoided detection, and it was imperative they continued to remain unspotted. If they were noticed now, they would be trapped in the city and easily rooted out like a fox flushed out of its hole by a pack of hunting dogs. The thought did nothing to cheer Zaria.

She looked upward, shading her eyes against the growing sunlight. She tried to search for dark silhouettes against the bright backdrop. They hadn't seen flying reindeer, or flying anything really, but Zaria wasn't going to dismiss the idea even if it did sound silly and childish. She knew the Wild Hunt would not stop until it had found its quarry – them.

A piercing noise ahead caught their attention. Aleks held up his hand to indicate they stop. The children stilled immediately. Zaria couldn't see anything past the boys, but their trepidation was palpable.

Aleks gestured to them again, as he took a right turn into an arcade styled structure. With the protection afforded by the roof, the children ceased glancing up in dread. They needed to keep moving, but to Zaria it seemed like they were running in circles and the towering stalagmites didn't help. Her view was too obscured to know where they were headed.

"How far?" Geirr asked Aleks when they stopped next at the top of a hilly part of the city.

"I don't know."

Geirr deflated. "We're not going to make it," he complained. "I'm tired. My feet hurt. And I'm hungry again."

Filip punched him. "Don't get all whiny on us now, Geirr. Nobody's spotted us."

Aleks tossed his hands up in the air and groaned. "Don't say that! We'll be doomed for sure!"

Zaria rolled her eyes. "Don't be such a goose, Aleks. Superstition is the last thing we need. Look!"

She pointed across the rooftops and it appeared the city ended. Darkness stretched in the distance with a faint twinkling of lights near what looked like a dock. Like a specter ghosting through the scene, an icy river skirted the edge of the troll city and disappeared into blackness. The lights from the mirrors did not reach this section of the cavern at this time of day.

Geirr said, "Thank God." His good humor didn't last and his voice took on a cynical note when next he spoke. "But we'll be exposed. They'll see us and capture us quickly out there."

"Over there," Filip said, pointing to the last of the buildings near the city's edge. "A sleigh. We can use that."

"A sleigh isn't going to do us much good," Geirr countered pessimistically.

Zaria tapped her chin thoughtfully. "A sleigh could work, especially if that river is as frozen as it appears to be."

"We'd need a team to pull it," Aleks said, getting excited.

"Wolves? You must be mad! They're wild animals. They're not sled dogs."

"The trolls tamed them," Zaria offered.

Geirr muttered in disgust. "That's not saying much."

"Take it easy, mate," Filip said. "We can do it."

Behind them the cacophony of noises rose. They all strained to hear how close the pursuit was. Aleks looked around puzzled.

He said, "I don't see where they're coming from. The noise echoes too much to pinpoint it anymore."

"It's echoing off the cave's walls," Geirr replied. He rolled his shoulders, stood up straight, and took a deep breath. "We should go, yes?"

Zaria grinned at him, happy he pulled himself out of his funk. "Let's go!"

The children raced down the street, whipped past the last major stalagmite tower, and aimed for the short squat building with the sleigh. A horn blew and howls turned into excited yips. Zaria gulped; she did not want to look behind her to see if they'd finally been spotted.

Filip however did look and yelled, "They just crested the hill!"

"DOWN THERE!" a deep troll voice boomed.

The responding roar from the mob of trolls would haunt Zaria's dreams for the rest of her life. She tripped on the uneven ground and went sprawling. Her hands stung, her knees throbbed, and she gasped in fright. Two pairs of strong arms hauled her to her feet and half-dragged- half-carried her the rest of the way as she struggled to limp along.

"Keep moving," Aleks said gruffly. "Don't stop. Don't slow down. Keep going."

"You can do it," Filip said on the other side of her.

Geirr raced ahead, he hurled open the barn doors and darted inside. As the trio reached the sleigh, Geirr raced out with two struggling reindeer. Their harnesses jingled loudly, adding to the wall of sound approaching them.

Aleks pushed Zaria up and got her into a seat, while Filip ran to help Geirr. Aleks joined them, and together the boys strong-armed the reindeer into place and hooked them to the sleigh. The animals reared in agitation from the noise, eyes wide with fear.

Zaria risked looking over her shoulder and moaned. The troll horde was bearing down on them. They had mere moments to escape. The wolves had sprung ahead of the trolls, snarling and yapping as they spread out to block escape routes.

The boys climbed into the sleigh and Aleks took the reins. "Ho!" he called, slapping them against the reindeer's backs.

The bucks lurched forward and the sleigh staggered along behind. Zaria held her breath and the edge of her seat as the conveyance began to pick up speed. But their start had been too slow. Wolves were yapping at their heels and the distance to the river seemed impossibly far.

"Hurry, Aleks, oh do hurry," Zaria called out.

"Ho!" he shouted, urging the reindeer to increase their pace with another slap of the reins against their backs.

The reindeer ran faster. Marginally. It was no use. Even fresh, the reindeer could not pull four children in a sleigh faster than unencumbered wolves could run, even when weary.

As the wolf pack grew closer, Filip and Geirr struggled to snap off the arms of the sleigh. Geirr almost fell out when one gave way, but Filip and Zaria managed to snag his jacket and haul him back into the safety of the sleigh.

The makeshift weapon was put to immediate use as a wolf leapt toward them. Geirr whacked it in the face. A pathetic whimper came from the beast, as it fell to the floor.

"Gotcha," he shouted in glee, holding his weapon over his head.

Zaria was tenderhearted enough to feel bad for the creature, but she had to be pragmatic. The wolves were attacking, and they needed to defend themselves. Softness was not what was needed now.

She and Filip broke the second arm off, and Filip flanked Geirr. The boys fought off the wolves' attacks with wild swings. Zaria's heart was in her throat, and she jumped whenever the snapping jaws grew too close.

It seemed that more and more wolves were joining the fray. They poured over the barren earth like a flood. The reindeer were slowing; the trolls gaining. Several whoops of triumph echoed in the dark as lantern lights swung crazily in the gloom.

Just then a new sound reached their ears followed by great gusts of wind. They looked up. Flying drunkenly above them were Norwick and Hector. Norwick looked battered and tired, but his keen eyes glowed in the dark with determination and fierceness. Hector tossed them a rope.

"Loose the reindeer. Hook the rope to the sleigh. Norwick will pull!" he shouted.

Zaria scrambled to help Aleks turn the reindeer loose, while Geirr and Filip battled with the lingering wolf pack. She and Aleks got the rope secured and tugged it tight for good measure.

"Ready!" she called up to Hector.

"Hang on!" he shouted.

She fell back against Aleks as the sleigh sprung forward. The distance between them and the wolves widened. Filip and Geirr crowed as the wolf pack fell back. Many of the ones they'd incapacitated were slowly regaining their feet. Some were stumbling still dazed from the boys' blows. A few wolves still lay on the ground.

The sleigh reeled as Norwick took a sharp turn. Filip and Geirr were tossed into their seats, as they heaved one way and then the next, skidding over the rough ground until with a thump they landed on the icy river.

"That was brilliant!" Filip yelled.

The boys whooped in triumph even as the troll horde howled in rage at their escape. Zaria watched them charge to the river's edge and stop. They cackled, hollered, stormed, and thundered. But Norwick was leaving them in the dust and soon the Wild Hunt was a prick of light in the distance.

"Why don't they chase us?" Zaria asked loudly, trying to be heard over the boys' enthusiasm.

"Because this frozen river belongs to Olaf," called Hector. "Two different kingdoms and nay do they cross, unless war is the goal."

Chapter Nine: Emerging into Álfheim

Hector and Norwick landed some hours later, careful to set down on the frozen river. The sleigh skidded to an uneasy stop. Pinpricks of light came down in shafts from the ceiling where natural holes allowed sunlight to slip through. It was still gloomy, but it wasn't completely dark.

Zaria was glad to stretch her legs. She hopped out first and ran over to their rescuers. She rubbed

Norwick's fur with affection. He nuzzled her head with his chin, as happy to see her as she him.

"Brave, strong, smart, wyvern," she told him, stroking his leg. The wyvern rumbled halfheartedly. "How is he?" she asked Hector, concerned.

He stared at Norwick for a long time. "His fire is gone and that does something to a wyvern."

"Will he get it back? One of those horrible trolls gloated about a dry ice bomb."

"It's possible he could," Hector said, moving over to Norwick and examining him. He stroked Norwick's neck, legs, and wings. "He wouldn't be worth much to the trolls, if he didn't have fire. So I can't imagine they used more than they needed to stop his flame in the first place."

"How soon before he recovers?" Zaria asked.

The others had joined them by this point. Filip reached out to the poor beast. "I hope he does," Filip said, scratching at Norwick's chest.

Geirr petted Norwick too and said, "He seems cooler than before."

"He is," Hector replied. "His internal fire is what keeps him warmest, although his fur helps. I'll have to keep an eye on him."

"You're all right," Zaria whispered to the creature, pressing a kiss to his snout. "You're with friends now. Rest."

Norwick nodded sleepily, liking this suggestion. He curled up on the ice, wrapping his wings around his body and tucking in his head. Geirr and Filip patted him a few more times and stepped away. Zaria followed Hector as the man moved around his pet, unloading and repacking items strapped on Norwick's back.

"So how did you escape?" Aleks demanded from the back.

Zaria shot him a look of disapproval, which he ignored. Filip and Geirr watched on in curiosity and wariness. It hadn't occurred to them to wonder if Hector's presence among them was a trick.

"Well?" Aleks repeated.

Hector stopped working on his packing and turned to face Aleks. In his hand was the stargazer, which he held out to the boy. Aleks took it with a mulish expression on his face. He obviously did not want to be thankful for its retrieval.

"Awfully convenient," he said, his eyes never leaving Hector's face.

"Just the opposite actually," Hector returned mildly. He stood with his feet apart, shoulders squared, and removed the antlered hood of his cloak. "What do you want to know?"

Aleks pressed another notch in the stargazer and it lit up. Beams of light shot through the star-shaped holes and illuminated the gloom around them. Zaria saw that the river lay close to one side of the cavern near the walled boundary.

"I want to know if you're here because you bargained for your freedom with the trolls and plan to steal what we have to retrieve for Olaf."

Hector stroked his blond beard idly. "If I did, would I tell you?"

Aleks' lips thinned in displeasure. "No, I suppose not. So I guess we're at an impasse." He looked at the others. "We should leave them and keep going."

"With what supplies?" Zaria asked, folding her arms. "Are we to travel on foot?"

Geirr nodded. "I know you don't like it, Aleks, but we don't have much choice."

"There's always a choice," Aleks said, waving the stargazer meaningfully at the others.

"I'm not human," Hector said. "I'm an ellefolken. Your toy will not work on me, nor would Norwick be of much use to you. He's not cut out to carry four people and he's in no condition to keep dragging your sleigh."

Aleks put down his hand. "You're a what? Elk-folk?"

"Aye. We're forest folk; we prefer living around alder trees. You could say my people are cousins with the elves of the Álfheim."

"What's a Stag Lord?" asked Filip. "I heard the trolls call you that at the palace."

"It means, I'm heir to the throne," said Hector. He shrugged. "Once I'm king I won't have the freedom to explore the realms. My duties will keep my movements considerably constricted. Boy," he continued, addressing Aleks. "If you must know I am damn good at trading. Trolls might be known for their trickery, but I am at my best when bargaining. I was already loosed before they realized that the trade I made with them was chicanery at its finest."

Aleks nodded. "What did you trade them for?"

"A secret way in and out of Queen Helena's realm without her shoes in exchange for my freedom, my beast's, and yours."

Geirr shook his head in disgust. "I still can't believe all this mess was because of some lady's footwear."

Hector smiled and turned back to his belongings. He rummaged for a moment before pulling out silver tinfoil packages. He handed them to the children. "They're MRE's. Meals-ready-to-eat," he explained. "Don't get me wrong they're nasty, but you humans certainly know how to provide sustenance in a pinch. We'll eat, rest, and make our way topside."

***

"Is Queen Helena your mother?" asked Zaria late afternoon.

She was ridiculously tired. Looking at the boys, she could see they felt the same, but each was determined to trudge up the sloping cave floor and reach the top. They were near Álfheim according to Hector and would emerge in its protected glades when they broke the surface.

"No," Hector replied. "She's a sorceress. She rules the Under Realm which stretches beyond the Gjöll River. The elves have aligned with her for generations. They guard the Gjöll and the Gjallarbrú – the bridge that spans this realm and connects to hers."

"It sounds like the River Styx in Greek mythology," Zaria said. "How fascinating!" And she was fascinated. This whole adventure was like watching a book come alive. What else was real?

"Why do the trolls need her shoes?" Geirr interrupted. He'd been listening quietly, focusing on the climb, but he was curious.

Hector guided Norwick gently by the snout. He looked at Geirr and said with solemnity, "You can't cross into her realm without a pair of her shoes."

The answer didn't satisfy Geirr, or Zaria for that matter. "Then why do the elves help guard her realm, if nobody can cross without them?"

"Because once you cross, you can't return to this realm without ridding yourself of them, which is nearly impossible. And nearly impossible is not impossible. There are members of her realm that we – elves, ellefolken, giants – don't want out. You wouldn't want them out either."

"Like who?" Filip asked, perking up a little. The conversation was finally getting interesting for him. He scratched his leg and swatted at a few gnats circling him.

"Dragons," Hector replied simply. "There's a reason there aren't any more in the world."

"No way," Filip said. "Cool. In another life, I could have been a knight with a noble steed."

Aleks shoved him forward, causing Filip to stumble. "Yeah right," he joked. "You wouldn't last five minutes in combat with a fire-breathing dragon."

Filip shoved Aleks back with a halfhearted, "Watch it."

Norwick extended a wing and flattened them both to the ground. Zaria and Geirr laughed. Even Hector looked amused.

"I'm glad to see you are getting your spirit back," Hector told the beast. "Dragons," he said to the children, "are shapeshifters. They can be man, elf, giant, troll, or beast. They are most powerful in their true form, but I wouldn't underestimate them in their secret forms."

Geirr said, "Do they have powers?"

"Not like Helena, who is a sorceress. If they could produce the magic that she could, we'd be in serious trouble. Their power is animal magnetism. They can charm; they can mesmerize; they can beguile and lead others so far astray that they are unrecognizable."

Zaria looked at him wide-eyed. "So how did you fight them?"

"You can't fight a dragon unless you are supremely aware of who you are, your identity, your autonomy, and your dominion over yourself. Otherwise a dragon can creep into your heart and mind like a poison and take you over, make you lose yourself. That is where their power comes from."

Zaria nodded numbly. "I'm glad they are trapped in the underworld."

"Under Realm," Hector corrected, placing a comforting hand on her shoulder. "You and me both, Princess."

"Why do you call her that?" Aleks asked. "Olaf called her that too."

"And one of the cave-trolls."

Hector jerked in surprise. "One of mountain-trolls called you princess?"

Zaria shrugged. "Mangus, the one that captured me… but not at first. At first he called me girl."

"That is serious," Hector said, stroking his beard thoughtfully. He looked behind them into the deep shadows of the cave. "We best hurry along then. If that troll tells King Kafirr who you are, our previous troubles with the trolls will seem minor by comparison."

"But who am I?" Zaria asked. "I'm nobody. I'm not a princess. I'm just a normal kid."

"That is not my secret to share. And even if I could share it, I would not."

"What does that mean?" Zaria asked.

When she didn't get a response she looked over at Aleks. He was similarly disturbed. They shared a meaningful look before hurrying to rejoin the group that had gotten slightly ahead of them.

***

"We're here," Hector said, as they reached a rock wall.

"Um," Zaria started. "Hector, this is a pile of rocks. Wouldn't that way make more sense?" She gestured to the left where the floor continued to slope up.

"Ye of little faith," he replied with a grin and a wink. "The elves are masters of illusions. Come, follow me."

He walked up to the wall, stuck his hand around a corner that was indistinguishable to the naked eye and then disappeared.

"That was cool," Geirr commented, awe in his voice. He followed next.

It reminded Zaria of her favorite fantasy series, but instead of the use of magic to slide into a wall it was optical illusion to slide around it. She waited to go through last, so she could appreciate the deception of the illusion. It was quite a treat to see Norwick slip through and then vanish like smoke. She went next and loved the discovery of the corridor behind the wall.

"Good," Hector said in the cramped space. "Now we go to the elevator."

"You're kidding? An actual elevator?"

Hector laughed. "No, of course not an elevator like the ones you are used to in your cities. This one does not use electricity."

The bad thing about being at the back of the group, Zaria thought as she walked, was the inability to see around Norwick. His bulk took up the entire hallway so she didn't see what caused the boys to murmur their appreciation. She heard it though. It was water; at first unrecognizable, but as they got closer it roared in her ears.

Hector shouted above the noise. "I'm going to talk to the guardian."

Zaria ducked between Norwick's feet and scrambled into a standing position. She blew her wisps of hair out of her eyes and gasped in delight. Twinkling lights lit the space all around. They moved with soft fluttering sounds and Zaria realized that they were fireflies. Hundreds of them!

A marvelous old wooden mechanical structure with wheels, gears, pulleys, buckets, and water filled the space from wall to wall. They stood at the banks of a natural waterfall which churned the dark water at their feet. The boys were exploring their surroundings with obvious glee. It was like stumbling upon a lost world.

Hector knocked on a fortified metal door. A few moments passed, and Hector knocked again. The peephole opened and beady eyes looked out.

"What's this? Who's there?" asked a squeaky and unfriendly voice.

"Master Brown," Hector called loudly. "It is I, Hector. I've brought some young friends with me. We are looking for passage to the topside."

The beady eyes glinted as they took in the children. "Go away! I don't deal with humans."

"Come now, Master Brown," Hector cajoled. "That is no way to be hospitable."

"NO!"

Hector winked at the children. "Well then, I guess we'll have to camp here until you decide you'd rather be rid of us. My wyvern loves to leave places really smelly, and he's had a bad case of indigestion recently. I can only imagine what that will be like for you."

"And I love to sing," Zaria piped up, catching onto Hector's plan.

She started singing as loudly as she could and was subsequently earsplittingly off key. Her caterwauling reverberated in the space which made it worse. The boys took their cue from her and started climbing on things and pulling at things and banging on things.

Master Brown's beady eyes widened in alarm. "No need to do that!" he shouted. "Stop! Stop!"

A series of clicks and clacks reverberated in the cavern as he unlocked the door, which creaked angrily on its hinges as he yanked it open. A short blue-skinned man stood on a stepstool breathing heavily. He skewered them with a spiteful glare. His mouth was pursed in a tight moue of repressed anger. Zaria immediately ceased her singing and gulped nervously.

"Sometimes, I really despise you, Hector."

"Now, now, Master Brown, don't be like that. We're all friends here."

Hector motioned to the three boys, and they quickly clambered down from their various perches. The children gathered meekly in front of Master Brown and Hector trying to look angelic. The illusion cracked as first Filip, then Aleks, then Geirr, and finally Zaria burst out laughing.

Master Brown harrumphed. He turned to Hector. "I was just about to turn in for the night. You and your group are proving to be awfully inconvenient. It's going to cost you."

Hector held out his hand and asseverated, "Of course. It is, after all, a great inconvenience to you. Shall I add two of your favorites to your next order? On me, of course?"

Master Brown's face lit with pleasure. "That would be satisfactory."

He shook Hector's hand to seal the deal and then hopped off his stool. He scurried around flipping switches, turning knobs, and checking gears. He cast a baleful look at Norwick and made a few more adjustments.

"There," he said satisfied with his work. "Now," he hurried over to the children and started to herd them onto a circular shape on the floor. "Stick close together if you please. Hang onto the rail."

"What rail?" Aleks said, looking around.

With a *swoosh* a rail sprung from the floor. It stopped at their waists. The children took a firm grip and shrieked, as the circular platform leapt to the ceiling propelled by a geyser of water.

Zaria ducked down because it looked like they were going to crash into the ceiling. Her whole body tensed at the expected impact. She focused on Hector and Norwick, as they watched from below, their shapes getting smaller and smaller.

Moonlight fell unexpectedly on the quartet, and Zaria looked up. Dirt and small stones rained down as the ceiling cracked open. The opening enlarged into a circle roughly double the size of their platform. Their ride stopped abruptly when they drew even with the opening.

"Oh wow," Aleks said, awed.

Zaria agreed. They were in the middle of a silver glade. The snow glittered, ice dripped like diamonds from tree branches, and birds chirruped like tinkling bells. It was surreal.

"Welcome to Álfheim," a male elf said from behind them. His ears were large and tapered into sharp points. At seeing them, Zaria mourned for a moment the fact that Aleks' ears did not do the same.

"Hello," Filip said with a small wave.

"It's not often that Master Brown admits visitors to us," the elf said, throwing a switch by his feet, which lowered the rail.

"Why is he called Master Brown?" Geirr asked. "He's blue."

The elf laughed. "You must be humans. He's a brownie. Brownies are blue. Master Brown is his name."

Geirr laughed through his embarrassment. "Oh," was all he said.

Zaria liked the elf's voice, which was smooth like maple syrup and just as rich. His hair was as pale a blond as Hector's hair was as dark a blond and still could be called blond. He had a trim mustache, a nicely folded cravat, starched shirt-points, and wore a friendly smile. His Victorian period clothing suited him. He held out his hand.

"Come," he said, helping the children off the platform one at a time. "My name is Edevart."

When the children were safely off the platform, Edevart picked up a hollow circular object and spoke into it. He placed it by his ear when he was done and nodded a few times. Then he spoke into it again.

"It's like a phone," Aleks said, surprised.

"Remember what Hector said?" Geirr said. He looked like he wanted to try the elf-phone himself. "Elves like to read and research human technology."

"That explains the water elevator too," Filip said, looking impressed. "Nifty."

Zaria was equally impressed. She continued gazing around trying to take it all in. There was so much to see. At her feet was a cluster of snow drops. She bent and plucked one, twirling it between her fingers.

"There we are," Edevart said, hanging up the phone.

The platform sank from view, and shortly after Hector and Norwick flew out of the opening.

Edevart laughed heartily. "I should have known it was you, Stag Lord. Welcome. Welcome."

Chapter Ten: Discovering Gloomwood Forest

The moon rose fully over the glades. There, situated high in the birch trees, silver lights winked on inside the elves' homes. The buildings and walkways were strung about like cobwebs, gossamer and shimmery. Frosted glass constructed most of the structures and Zaria could vaguely see the shadows of the occupants inside.

A bonfire was set up in the heart of the glade. There Zaria rested peacefully with the boys enjoying the warm glow thrown by the fire. She was happy, relaxed, and overly stuffed, but she wasn't complaining per se. Sleep tugged at her consciousness and her eyelids felt heavy, but Zaria fought it off. There was still too much to do to find Christoffer and time was running short.

"I hope Christoffer is okay," she said softly so only her friends could hear her.

Geirr rubbed his eyes and yawned. "We made it this far. It seems more and more doable each day."

Filip tossed a stick into the flames. The fire cast his face in flickering waves of light and shadows. He was brooding. Every now and then he looked about with a contemplative expression. Finally he sighed noisily and leaned forward on his haunches.

"Guys," he whispered, and Zaria had to lean closer to hear him. "This place is the least gloomy vale in the whole of Norway. Everyone is happy. The trees are healthy. Nothing is dark. Everything is silvery and shiny and glows."

Aleks looked around as if just realizing this and cursed. "You're right."

"But this is where Olaf directed us to go," Zaria said. "We have to be in the right place."

"Well," Geirr interrupted, dragging out the word. "If I recall correctly he said we should seek Álfheim for more about the heart, not necessarily that Álfheim was situated in Gloomwood Forest."

"But elves guard the dead," Zaria pressed. "It would make sense that we're somewhere in Gloomwood." She turned to face Aleks and said, "I wish Hector had thought to get all of our belongings from those trolls, not just your stargazer and his things."

Aleks shook his head. "I can live without the other stuff, but this little guy –" he held up the stargazer, "– will save our bacon."

"I could really use those maps," Zaria bemoaned; then continued with the non sequitur, "I'm so full."

Filip groaned and stretched out. "Me too. I don't think I could eat again for days. Those MRE's that Hector gave us and then the feast the elves heaped on us was way too much."

"I could sleep for a week," Aleks muttered, cracking his jaw on a yawn.

"We can do that once we get back home," Geirr suggested. "That way we could recover, and our parents would be none the wiser."

"Children," Hector called. He crossed the clearing and stood before them. "I've made arrangements with Edevart and his wife to host you this evening. If you need me, I plan to stick around a few days before moving on to Jötunheim."

Aleks and Geirr both asked why he was delaying his trip. Hector cocked his head to the side, regarding them. It was a funny look, and Zaria couldn't repress a giggle. The antlers on his head were the perfect added touch.

Hector ignored her giggling. "I'm having Norwick looked at by the head husbandman. I want to make sure he's all right; give him a few days to recover."

"Oh," Aleks said.

Zaria looked at Hector anxiously. "You'll let us know, won't you?"

He nodded. "Of course, Princess. I know you and Norwick are friends. Goodnight now." He pointed in the direction he'd come from and moved away from the quartet. "You'll find Edevart over there."

***

Edevart and his wife, Frida, were excellent hosts. The friends each had a warm nest of blankets and pillows to sleep in. Frida was as open and friendly as a chattering magpie. Her hair was bright red, freckles danced across her cheeks, and her nose was smudged with flour. She bustled about the inside of the glass home as she heated water for tea and cakes.

Edevart sat at a beautifully carved table. The legs of the table featured various groups of deer running through the woods. Filip was fascinated and kept tracing the antlers of one with the pad of his thumb.

"Where did Hector find you all?" Frida asked when she finally paused between her discourse on traveling in winter and the history of her tea cakes (which involved her mother, and Silje, the elf queen). She handed them each a mug before picking up the teakettle to pour.

"His wyvern found us," Filip said between mouthfuls of cake, as he pointed to himself and Aleks. Apparently he had room for dessert after all, but Zaria didn't. She'd pop if she ate anything else.

"Yeah," Aleks said, "Terrified the cra– uh… stuffing out of us."

"And then Norwick found us," Zaria said, pointing to Geirr and herself.

"I bet meeting a creature like Norwick for the first time was a little unnerving," Frida said, sitting down with them and pouring a tea for herself.

"More than a little," Geirr grumbled. He waved away Frida's offer of tea cakes. "Full," he offered as an apology.

"I remember when Hector first got Norwick," Edevart said, his gaze faraway.

Aleks took a long swallow of tea and said, "He mentioned the previous owner didn't rub along with Norwick."

Edevart snorted. "That's an understatement. Per is a usually levelheaded husbandman, but Norwick was so stubborn and intractable that Per lost his temper with the beast on multiple occasions. Everyone knows a calm demeanor works best with wyverns."

"He didn't hurt Norwick, did he?" Zaria asked, aghast.

Frida rushed to reassure her. "We wouldn't be as good with beasts and creatures of the woods if we didn't respect the animals. Gentle hands, firm methods, fast results as my mother always said."

Aleks said, "Hector was helping us reach Álfheim, but we really need to reach Gloomwood."

"Gloomwood?" Edevart asked, puzzled. "Why would you children be interested in Gloomwood?"

"We're rescuing a friend," Filip said, reaching over to steal a cake from Aleks' plate.

"You don't want to go to Gloomwood Forest," Frida said, gathering cups and plates. She was clearly discomposed.

"Why not?" Zaria asked.

"Because chances are you will die," Edevart said with a note of finality. He then shooed them off to bed and wouldn't answer any further questions on the matter.

***

The next day was the fourth day of their adventure. Cleverness was running short amongst the four friends. They needed to know more about Gloomwood, and their elven hosts were not forthcoming with information.

At breakfast, which was served in a communal style with all of the elves coming and going as they pleased, the children squabbled about what to do next. In the end a straightforward approach was decided. They would target the younger looking elves to see what they would divulge in gossip about the forest.

Geirr, the one who had drawn the short straw, stood up to get unwanted seconds. Zaria and the others watched his progress. He did not look calm and was jittery with unspent energy. Zaria thought he probably wasn't the best choice, but she didn't want to have to ask either. It seemed almost forbidden.

While the cooks served him another bowl of an oatmeal-like substance, the group could see him talking to a white-haired girl elf. She gave him a strange look and wandered off. Geirr looked back at them, his face tense and unsmiling. Zaria gave him an encouraging smile.

Geirr joined the line for meat and stood behind two strapping young lads with bows across their shoulders. They seemed more interested in talking to Geirr than the elf girl. Zaria was hopeful.

If they didn't shut him down, he would soon casually mention the heart. Geirr would then try to draw the answers out of those around him about what it was and where it could be found. Zaria was more and more hopeful that Geirr was getting answers the longer it took for him to return.

About fifteen minutes later, Geirr sat down at the table with cold mush and a grin. Aleks took the slab of meat off his bowl and started to tuck into it. He liked venison.

"Well?" Filip asked, impatient. He flicked a piece of bread at Aleks' head and grinned when Aleks glared.

Zaria sat up and tossed her braids over her shoulder. Filip stopped playing with his food and looked expectantly at Geirr. Aleks also stopped eating to pay attention.

"Gloomwood Forest is a four hour trip to the west by foot. I didn't get much information about the heart other than it could be found in a circular vale of alder trees."

"Alder trees?" Zaria questioned, scrunching her nose and twirling a lock of hair around her finger. "Didn't Hector say his people lived by alder trees? Do you think we have to steal from Hector's people?"

Geirr looked at Zaria and shook his head. "The elves didn't say so. If the ellefolken live in Gloomwood Forest, it was never said."

Aleks looked up at the sky. "We need to get going soon then. It's already past mid-morning."

"There's one more thing," Geirr said, now looking a little worried. "Gloomwood Forest is home to ghouls, witches, banshees, and other creatures associated with evil and darkness."

"Which would explain Edevart's and Frida's reluctance to give us information," Zaria interjected.

Geirr shrugged. "Apparently these creatures are attracted to the underworld –"

"Under Realm," Zaria corrected. "Hector said it was the Under Realm."

"Er… right. Anyway, the elves give these creatures leeway in Gloomwood if they don't cause trouble. The elves mentioned the elders don't want to another start another war. The last one devastated the elves and ellefolken."

"Did you learn anything else?" Aleks asked.

Geirr shook his head. "Just that we need to be exceptionally careful, even though the elves regularly patrol the woods to keep the peace."

Zaria nodded, a thoughtful expression on her face. She picked up a loaf of bread and stuffed it in the waistband of her jeans.

"Really?" Filip said, giving Zaria an incredulous look.

She stuck her tongue out at him. "We'll either use the bread as breadcrumbs like in fairy tales or to stuff our ears so we don't hear the banshees wail."

"In that case –" Aleks stuffed a half loaf in his waistband, "– it doesn't hurt to have more."

***

It was some time before the changes to the forest were noticed by the children. They'd been too concerned about sneaking out from under Hector's watchful presence to see the first telltale signs that they had entered Gloomwood Forest. The bright silvery trees that made up the Álfheim grew scarred and gnarled. Shadows from the branches flickered like ghostly fingers along the ground. It was difficult to imagine that a few short hours ago they had sat down for breakfast in the cheery vale.

When they had first reached the west wall of trees outside Álfheim, the children stopped to pick up large hefty sticks. At first, the idea was to use them as weapons if the need arose, but the more pressing need for them was for leverage to wade through the snow.

Wading through thick snow wasn't anyone's idea of fun. Filip and Geirr bemoaned the absence of the snowshoes Hector had provided them, which like most of their gear, resided underground in Trolgar, the mountain-troll kingdom.

Zaria tried not to complain. It wouldn't do any good. So she studied their surroundings. Gloomwood Forest definitely earned the name. Even with most of the trees bare and covered in snow, the woods were decidedly gloomy. The shadows made creepy shapes that formed and dispersed in a blink on the ground and at a distance.

The trees looked rotten and the smell wafting from them was putrid. Some trunks even appeared to have faces trapped in them, screaming terror. It unnerved Zaria greatly, but she didn't say anything to the boys, thinking they would make fun of her.

A howl in the distance alerted the group. Aleks reached for his bread, but Zaria stayed his hand. She cocked her head to the side and listened. When it came again, accompanied by a horn, her eyes widened.

"The Wild Hunt!" she exclaimed.

Filip and Aleks cursed.

Geirr looked around worriedly. "Are you sure?" he asked. "I mean are you really, really, sure?"

The horn blasted again, louder. Zaria didn't need to corroborate her assumption anymore for they were all convinced. Geirr growled in frustration. She silently agreed with him. They did not need this now.

"Stay close," was all the warning Aleks gave before he took off at a run.

Once again the friends were going to rely on his sense of direction. Filip grabbed Zaria's hand and started hauling her forward. She grabbed Geirr's arm on the way past.

They ran, and as they ran, left behind tracks so large even the dumbest dog could have followed them. Crashing noises in the woods immediately behind them spurred the children on. There was no time to think. No time to plan. And apparently no time to run.

The Wild Hunt which had sounded distant was not as distant as the children had hoped. Glowing eyes from wolves appeared in the shadows. Growls and snarls and excited yips hedged them in from both sides. The call of the horn grew closer.

Aleks took swift action and charged at a singular set of glowing eyes. The wolf snapped at them, but Aleks whacked its snout with his walking stick. They raced past the wounded wolf and toward a burbling brook. Aleks leapt over a log and they all copied him as if they were playing a deadly game of follow-the-leader. Do or get left behind.

But the wolves and the shouts and the horn were just a distraction from the true hunting party. Ahead of them was Jorkden seated proudly on a harnessed brown bear. His white fur cloak rippled in the wind, and the grin on his face was so wide you could see he had tusks. Zaria hadn't noticed that before. He held up his spear.

"Found her," he called out. Then, "Groul, Yorgish, Mangus."

Another three trolls melted from the shadows. One was thick and stout with a scraggly beard, another tall and reed thin with a whip-like tail, and the last was between them in appearances with bushy brows. The last one was Mangus and he wore a mean expression. Clearly he was happy with how events had played out.

Zaria gave him her best stink-eye. He grinned in response. That grin was terrifying. She huddled closer to Filip, who stepped in front of her. Aleks and Geirr pushed closer too.

The boys held their sticks up, eager to fight as only untried teens could be. Zaria kept her stick braced against the ground. She was not eager to fight. She was tired of fighting and she was tired of running.

"Bring her to me," Jorkden said. His voice was quiet and more sinister because of it.

Zaria tripped on her own feet trying to back away. Filip righted her and pushed her away from him and the others.

"Run, Zaria," he urged. "Run and don't look back."

"I can't!" she cried.

A blast of sound erupted from the three trolls. They charged forward roaring and brandishing their spears. She couldn't leave the boys, she just couldn't. She was scared.

"Go now," Aleks yelled, and then he did a brave and utterly senseless thing and charged at the trolls.

Filip pushed her again, and she stumbled away. He watched her right her balance. Then, he pointed to the trees opposite them. "Now, Zaria, run."

She ran. When she reached the first set of trees she dared to look behind her and winced. The boys were being pummeled. Geirr had already lost his stick.

From the corner of her eye she saw Jorkden surge forward on his bear. She turned away and kept running. She crashed wildly through the trees. The woods got denser. The snow grew deeper. The smell grew fouler. She fell into a soft patch, losing her walking stick in the process.

The bear roared behind her. She struggled against the snow and dared not to look again. She'd be paralyzed in fear, if she saw Jorkden and the bear stalking her.

"Think, Zaria, think," she whispered to herself when she regained her feet.

Her gaze darted everywhere. She thought about climbing the trees, but knew she didn't have the coordination. She couldn't keep running willy-nilly either.

To her right the woods grew even closer; bushes with thick brambles were densely packed between the tree trunks. If she could reach them, perhaps she could hide in them. It would force Jorkden to relinquish his advantage on the bear. He'd have to get off and follow her, and he was bigger than the average troll. The going wouldn't be easy for him.

Just as the troll and bear lunged into view, she made her move. Plunging into the thicket, Zaria pressed forward. She ignored the scrapes and scratches the brambles and thorns inflicted on her. Behind her she heard Jorkden curse loudly. His bellowing spurred her on.

Deeper and deeper she went until like a cork she popped free into a golden glade. It was as gold and shimmery as the elves' glade was silver. The sunlight was so pure it looked like it had gilded the trees. There was no snow here. The sun had melted it all.

Across from her stood a young elk by a sluggish river. He had a white pelt and golden horns. He could have been the brother to the stag that had become Hector's cape. He was beautiful.

His bleak expression turned her heart over. Why was such a creature so sad? Zaria approached, forgetting for a moment her pursuer. She came within a few feet of the elk and stretched out her hand.

He snorted. The hot breath from his nostrils warmed her fingers. She ran her hand over his snout and down over his back. His fur was soft as velvet and as luxurious. She felt him breathe.

"You're magnificent," she told him.

He blinked slowly at her, his mouth twisted in an unhappy moue. His large eyes seemed to hold the whole world in them and silently say it was too much of a burden to bear. His eyes were golden like his antlers, and she could see her reflection in them. What must he think of her presence?

"I'm in trouble," she said. "The Wild Hunt is after me, and I don't know why. My friends are in danger, and our other friend is being ransomed by a river-troll. What do I do?"

Of course the elk said nothing. How could he? She felt silly for expecting an answer. Too many fairy tales, she thought. But he looked so wise she couldn't help the asking. She cast her gaze at the river and frowned. Knives flowed in it. Actual knives – with blades and handles!

She stroked the creature quietly for a moment while she pondered the strange vision. When she returned her caresses to his neck she noticed he wore something. Hooking her fingers around the chain she lifted it up and stared in shock.

In her hands was a rough ebony stone shaped somewhere between and arrow and a heart. She unclasped it and held it aloft. When the sunlight pierced it the stone turned white.

She looked around and noticed that the golden glade was circular. The trees were not misshaped like in the rest of Gloomwood Forest. They stood tall and proud with branches interlocked with one another. You could not tell where one ended and another began.

The trunks were thick and old, their roots deep. They too had face-like images held within their depths, but these faces were noble somehow and watchful. That kind of gave her the creeps too. She looked away.

Somehow she'd made it to the heart of Gloomwood Forest. And in her possession was the heart of the forest itself, she was sure of it. She grabbed the elk's face in her hands. He pranced away in discomfort, but she held him until he settled.

"Can you help me? I need to get to the Glomma."

His intelligent eyes weighed her and he nodded.

"Thank you," she said, bussing his nose.

He knelt, and she clambered onto his back. She tied the necklace around her neck then gave him a pat to indicate she was ready. Together they turned, followed the river and exited the glade in the opposite direction she'd entered.

Chapter Eleven: Fleeing the Hunt

Zaria and the stag reentered the main part of the forest where the river sliced through the glade. Flashes of silver light from the knives bounced off the shadows and brightened the surrounding gloom. All was silent except for the sound of the water.

The elk took a path that was set at an angle from the river, turning them southeast. His feet were sure and his pace steady. He did not seem afraid which heartened Zaria tremendously, but she still scanned the woods like Hector had taught her a few days ago. Just in case.

The further away they got from the river the more sounds of life returned. Trees groaned under the weight of snow, icicles clinked in the wind, and the roar of water faded into the white noise of the forest's inhabitants resuming normal behaviors.

Night fell and still she and the elk wandered. The bite in the air grew chillier. Zaria briskly rubbed her gloved hands and stuffed them under her armpits. She hunched down and watched her breath fog for a few minutes.

A sharp crack resounded in the dark. She and the elk froze. He cocked his head listening carefully to the sounds in the woods. All had gone silent, hushed by the unexpected sound. He pawed the ground nervously, but otherwise stayed still.

Zaria peered into the forest behind her, regarding the shadows intently. She clutched the stone hanging from her neck and prayed for guidance. Should they continue moving forward or stop for the night?

"How much farther, buddy?" she asked, stroking his neck. "Do you need to take a break? I think I might."

He hunkered down allowing her to get off. When she clambered down, she groaned. Stretching was both a delicious joy and a torture as she worked her stiff muscles and relaxed her posture.

She kicked at the snow until she formed a bit of a nest. When she'd made space big enough for the two of them she sat down. Zaria felt a bit ridiculous sitting at the elk's feet with him peering down at her curiously. She patted the earth beside her.

"Join me," she said softly.

The elk circled twice and curled up beside her, lending her his warmth. She snuggled into his fur and breathed in his rich earthy scent. For a while she lay there quietly looking up at the stars through the branches. They twinkled brightly, and those friendly lights combined with the stag's warmth made her feel safe. She fell asleep, guarded by her mysterious woodland creature and the sky.

***

Before dawn broke, Zaria was nudged awake by the stag. He waited dutifully for her while she made a quick trip into the woods to relieve her bladder. When she returned, she saw him pulling up hunks of the scruffy vegetation she revealed under the snow the night before.

She was feeling a bit hungry herself and nibbled at the bread she'd carried yesterday. It was stale and gross. She made a face, but then forced herself to keep eating it. Even stale bread was better than nothing on an empty stomach.

As her companion continued to eat, Zaria looked around and noticed for the first time that they appeared to be out of Gloomwood Forest. She'd missed the changing of the trees last night. Gone were the ugly gnarled trees and now all around them were cheerful alders, birches, and spruces.

She fingered the necklace she'd appropriated from the elk yesterday. While tracing the cord she absently bounced on the balls of her feet. She was anxious to get moving. She wanted to rescue Christoffer and find her other friends. The elk stopped eating to stare at her.

"Do we have long to reach the Glomma?"

He went back to pulling up the grasses. Zaria wrinkled her nose but left him alone. If the journey was long he would need his strength. She plucked a dripping icicle from a low hanging branch and greedily lapped at it.

A crack echoed in the forest. It came at the same pitch and resonance as the one last night. Zaria swiveled around trying to pinpoint the spot it came from. It had sounded much closer than last night.

The elk nudged at her insistently, which she took as a hint to get going fast. She clambered onto his back and they were off, flying through the trees. He clearly knew something she did not.

A howl raised gooseflesh on her arms. Zaria gasped. It couldn't be!

"Oh no!" she moaned, clutching at the elk's fur. "Please no."

A horn blew and a din of noise rose up from behind her. Zaria shook her head in disbelief. The Wild Hunt was after her again. Again! She knew they never stopped until their quarry was captured or killed. If only she'd been wrong about that like she'd been about gullibility in trolls.

"Hurry, friend," she called to him, leaning over his neck, making herself as small as possible.

And hurry he did. They raced toward the rising sun. They darted through trees, clambered over hilly terrain, scampered down sloping valleys, leapt over fallen logs, and ducked under branches. He flew through the landscape as if the hounds of hell were chasing them.

Zaria clung to him for dear life. His run was not a smooth canter like a horse, but his feet were sure and they seemed to be keeping the same distance between them and the hunt. As long as they could do that they could reach the Glomma safely.

Spine-tingling howls and wolf calls echoed all around them in the crisp morning. The elk did not seem to be terrified of them. His pace was determined. He ran without ceasing, and he paused not when the echoes made it seem like they were surrounded.

Zaria looked behind them to confirm their pursuers were nowhere in sight. She spooked when she saw shadowy forms agilely skirting around obstacles. The wolf pack was gaining ground.

She quickly faced front again and squeezed her eyes shut and prayed. She concentrated on the movement of the elk under her. The rhythm lulled her fears. But then he abruptly stopped.

Jerking upright, Zaria glanced around wildly. The elk pranced in agitation under her. Ahead of them dark inkblots melded in and out of the blinding sunlight and slowly coalesced into terrifying snarling forms. The wolves had cleverly surrounded them.

A bugling sound ripped from the stag's throat, a clear warning. The wolves hesitated briefly before cautiously creeping closer, repositioning for attack, readying to pounce.

When the attack came, the wolf launched at them from their left side. Gnashing teeth and gleaming eyes filled Zaria's vision. The elk blocked it by knocking it away with his antlers, and nearly knocking her to the ground too. Her heart beat frantically, as the urge to flee clawed its way through her.

Another wolf leapt at them. Zaria shrieked when the elk lunged forward and knocked it backward with a blow from his golden antlers. A wolf snapped at their heels. The stag kicked backward hitting its snout. It was like riding a bucking bronco, but the ride lasted longer than eight seconds. Her teeth jarred in her head.

Then, her friend and protector yelped, prancing in an uneasy circle. She looked down and kicked at a wolf who'd managed to sink its teeth into one of the elk's haunches. The wolf let go instantly, whining.

An opening appeared in the wolves' ranks, and the elk attacked. He swept two wolves back using his antlers and charged for the opening that would be their escape. They eked through two springing wolves and plunged to freedom.

Zaria heard how heavy the stag breathed. His breath fogged thickly in the morning air. She worried about the blood running down his legs dotting the snow-covered ground.

She heard the wolves pursuing, and another horn blasted. Looking back she saw the wolves slow and stop. They disappeared from view. Zaria didn't know if she should be relieved or worried. What would be coming for them next?

Steadying her nerves, she patted the stag encouragingly. Whispering to the noble creature calmed her racing heart. She said many nonsensical things, telling him how strong and brave he'd been. She clutched the necklace in her hand until the sharp edges pierced her skin. They had to be close. They just had to be.

Snow began to fall. The fat white flakes were slow at first, but then built into a stinging flurry. The weather would help hide their escape. It would cover their tracks, maybe even their smell. Wind whispered through the trees and the clinking of icicles grew to a steady clamor. A white-breasted owl screeched, as it took to the sky, startling the pair.

The stag huffed and slumped. Zaria shook him gently. Her limbs felt heavy as the tension left her. "Don't give up," she urged. "We can't stop now."

The creature's golden horns dipped downward. He was exhausted. Zaria realized that wolves were sent to wear him down, to allow the rest of the hunting party to catch up to them. She jumped off his back and marched in front of him. She grabbed his face, and this time he didn't protest, merely huffed. His warm breath slid over her face.

Snow clung to him. She brushed it off, stroking his snout tenderly. "I know you're tired," she whispered. "I'm tired too, but we have to keep moving."

The stag whined in protest. Zaria stroked his neck and sides. She examined his leg. It was still bleeding. She looked around for something to staunch the flow and seeing none didn't know what to do. But then an idea came to her. Zaria ripped the cord out of the neck of her hoodie and tied it tightly above the wound.

"That'll have to do," she told him. "If we don't get moving the wolves will be back and their masters too."

A shiver raced down her back. Zaria glanced around looking for the source. Across from her through the flurry emerged a squad of trolls riding great big brown bears. She gulped.

"Too late," she whispered. "They found us."

The stag whined and nipped her shoulder. She chanced a look at him. His big caramel-gold eyes gazed at her earnestly. He nipped her again. She didn't hesitate; she scrambled onto his back as he took off.

"After them!" bellowed one of the trolls.

A horn blast sounded, and the woods erupted in chaos. Zaria and the stag zigzagged through charging bears, flashing weapons, and snapping jaws. Zaria didn't see how they were going to make it this time. Not surrounded as they were. But the elk moved with jerky determination, flanks, antlers, and hooves carrying them forward.

The tree line broke, and Zaria cried out in joy. Ahead was a river. She hoped it was the Glomma and that at last they had made it. She hunkered down and urged the elk forward. Her vision tunneled. They'd be safe if they could make it to the water. Ice flows floated by on its currents.

Without warning Zaria was knocked off the back of the stag. She landed sprawled in the snow. The elk kept running, splashing into the freezing cold water. He stopped as if realizing he'd lost his charge. Prancing in a circle he turned back to face her. He moved back to the bank.

"No," she shouted to him, scrambling onto her hands and knees. "Stay back!"

She lurched forward, only to have her feet yanked from under her. Kicking frantically with her feet, Zaria's gaze connected with her attacker. A female troll with bulging eyes cackled at her. She kicked again, landing a connecting blow to the troll's nose. The troll howled in pain, letting Zaria go to clutch her wounded nose.

Zaria was on her feet running toward the stag. Another troll crossed her path. He was burly and carried a multipronged spear. She darted left and he angled his body to block. She darted right, and he repositioned again. Zaria feinted and dove under his legs, skidding headfirst into the water.

She gasped in shock, surging to her feet. Icy water cascaded down her entire body. But she shouted with joy, making her way to the elk. They'd done it. They were safe.

"Come here, Princess," sneered the troll she'd dodged.

"Not a chance!" Zaria shouted back. She hugged the elk, kissing his snout. "You did it, you big beautiful beast."

"Hand her over, Olaf," Jorkden called out as he emerged from the other side of the river.

Zaria spied her friends walking out of the tree line. Filip waved sheepishly at her. His face was scraped pretty badly and one of his eyes was swollen shut. Aleks didn't look too much better. He leaned heavily on Geirr, favoring his right leg. Geirr's nose was busted and a trickle of blood dripped down the side of his mouth.

Behind them Yorgish, Groul, and Mangus prodded the boys forward with spears. Other trolls joined them. Soon both sides of the river were crowded with trolls. They yelled and hollered, taunting and saying ugly things.

"Olaf," Jorkden shouted. "Stop hiding."

"I be not hiding," the river-troll jeered nearby. "Jorkden be lacking sight."

Zaria whirled around to face him. He stood in the water, still in rags and oblivious to the cold. His blue-brown scales shone wetly as if he'd just emerged from the river. Perhaps he had.

Chapter Twelve: A Bargain Completed

"The little princess be having honor after all," Olaf said, a pleased expression twisting his ugly features into an even uglier visage. "I knew I could be counting on you doing what be needed to save your friend."

"Where is Christoffer?" Zaria demanded.

The boys shouted the same thing from the sidelines along the bank of the river. She grimaced when a troll, Yorgish or Groul, whacked Filip on the head. He scowled back and set his mouth in a mulish line, but quieted.

"Hand over the princess," Jorkden commanded.

Olaf didn't even look at the mountain-troll. "No. She possesses something I desire."

Olaf stalked over to her. Zaria held her ground, her hand tightly over the necklace. She wouldn't give it to him until Christoffer was safe. She narrowed her eyes at him.

"You didn't answer me," Zaria said when he stood a foot from her, her elk friend between them.

She studied Olaf. He looked much the same. He was still wicked thin with long limbs and slender webbed fingers. His big ears dwarfed his face and his clothes were still tattered and bald. There was something different though. Zaria couldn't quite put her finger on it.

She glanced him over again. His perpetually unhappy expression looked odd for some reason. It dawned on her the reason his expression looked odd was because it was happy. Not just happy, gleeful. It gave Zaria the creeps.

"No friend of Princess' until I be in possession of the Hart," Olaf admonished.

Zaria stepped around the elk and squared off against him. "No."

"No?" Olaf said, incredulously. His black eyes narrowed in anger. "No is not a word the little princess wishes to say to me."

"Just hand her over," Jorkden sneered. He made a move to step into the water. "She is not your concern. Kafirr wishes to see her."

Olaf shot him a look of pure contempt. "I not be at full strength, Jorkden, but I be strong enough to make you and your trolden suffer. Do not push me."

Jorkden's foot hesitated just above the waterline. Then with determination he placed it in the water. And then he stepped in with his other foot, planting himself defiantly on Olaf's territory.

"I have my king's orders, river-troll," Jorkden said. "The princess is ours as a captive of the Hunt."

"Your actions be breaking Kafirr's and mine's treaty," Olaf warned. "Leave now while I still let you and believe your actions to be impulsive and something to be ignored."

"Grab her," Jorkden yelled, gripping his spear and shifting his stance.

His brigade surged into the water, splashing loudly and yelling ferociously. The wolves and bears stayed behind on the shore. Jorkden pulled back his spear arm and tossed the weapon at Olaf. Zaria ducked instinctively.

She heard a sharp cracking crystalline sound. Looking up she gaped in disbelief. Olaf hadn't moved an inch. His disdainful expression was familiar. In front of him the spear the mountain-troll threw was held aloft, immobilized by a wave of frozen water. Jorkden's expression was grim.

Zaria looked at the boys who had been abandoned on the snowbank. They were busily working on the ropes that held them tied together. Her gaze snapped back to the mountain-trolls as their cries and curses rang out in alarm. Some were terrified, their eyes rolling wildly and arms flailing. Like the spear, the trolden had been frozen in place, their feet held in ice blocks.

"Tsk. Tsk," murmured Olaf.

He plucked the spear out of the air and tossed it back at Jorkden. The mountain-troll tried to dodge and fell backwards, landing awkwardly because he couldn't move his feet. The spear soared passed him.

Olaf stood over Jorkden, watching him with a nasty expression. He bent over and plucked at Jorkden's wet and soggy fur vest. When his warty nose was an inch away from Jorkden, Olaf flashed his yellow toothy smile as nasty as Zaria had ever seen him.

"Kafirr controls his mountain and be making it grow your homes. I control my waters. Jorkden of Trolgar, the Dragomir Treaty between us be broke by your actions."

"You won't get away with this," Jorkden spat, his face flushing red with anger even as he sweated.

Olaf dropped him with a splash and laughed, swinging back to Zaria. "I shall flood Trolgar and trap all the deserters in ice. Then with your pathetic excuse of a troll race eradicated I will be gifting Trolgar to Koll and his army."

A roar of impotent rage burst from Jorkden. His trolden stopped moaning and stared at him. They clearly missed what was said between Olaf and their leader. Zaria watched in silence as Jorkden's rage faded into bleakness.

Olaf stood before Zaria again. He clapped his hands together. "Where were we? Ah yes, Princess is to be handing over the Hart or her friend be trapped forever in slavery to dwarves."

"Not until I see Christoffer," she said stubbornly.

Olaf tilted his head. "You not be in position to be making demands, Princess."

Zaria folded her arms. Her ankles were wet and freezing. She was tired. She was hungry. She was not amused.

"Are we at an impasse?" she asked Olaf. "I have what you want, but I will not hand it over until I see the whites of Christoffer's eyes."

"That will be tough, Princess," Olaf said silkily. "He be safely hidden away near Fredrikstad."

"Not my problem," Zaria replied. "I met the criteria of your demands. I am here with the heart and I want my friend. How do you propose to confirm with me Christoffer's freedom and safety?"

She looked over at the boys. Filip gave her a thumbs-up. The others nodded. She had their support. No bargain would be completed without all parties present.

Olaf mulled things over quietly, looking at her elk companion. Finally he said, "How about a compromise, Princess?"

"No way!" Aleks shouted. "No more bargains!"

Olaf held a hand up to silence him. He kept his gaze fixed firmly on Zaria. "I will show you that your friend be safe. I will also show you his release. I not be bringing him here. It be not so easy to do."

"How can you do that?" she asked, suspicious.

Olaf cackled and bent low. He trailed a single finger in the water. The water sprung up and shaped a clear pedestal with a bowl. It looked sort of like a birdbath if a birdbath was lopsided and covered in spikes. He beckoned Zaria closer. She splashed over with reluctance. She did not want to stand near him.

"Look here," he told her and pointed to the water in the crystalline bowl.

She looked and gasped.

"What is it?" Filip called out. He budged Aleks forcefully away as his friend tried to lean over him for a better look.

"I see Christoffer," she shouted back. Her face split into a grin. "He's all right."

Geirr frowned. "How do we know this is really Christoffer? And that you're showing him as he is now?"

Olaf scoffed. "Do you think to be communicating with him? This be a parlor trick, not a way to communicate. I be able to show anything in my territory with water from my river."

"I don't like it," Aleks said. He didn't trust Olaf and frankly neither did Zaria.

Olaf glared at him. "Princess," he spit out. "Do you agree to complete the bargain? Will you hand over the Hart?"

Zaria bit her lip. She looked for help from the boys. Filip shrugged. Aleks shook his head. Geirr frowned. She looked back into the bowl at Christoffer. His surroundings were indistinct and featureless. He looked bored, but unharmed. Zaria looked at Olaf and nodded.

"You must be saying it out loud," Olaf prodded, reaching out eagerly.

"Don't be a fool," Jorkden warned her, some of his verve returning.

"You not be speaking," Olaf growled. "Princess, say it. Complete the trade and your friend be freed. Do not, and I will hand him over to the slave markets."

While Zaria hesitated, Jorkden sat up with a splash and with a grunt of triumph pulled a foot free from its icy trap. His skin was blue and dark from frostbite.

He'd lost his shoe; it was still stuck in the remains of the ice block.

Jorkden's freedom was short-lived as Olaf used his river to push the troll under the waters. Zaria was horrified. She couldn't watch it.

She shouted, "Olaf, I agree to complete the bargain. The heart of Gloomwood Forest for the freedom and safety of my friend, Christoffer."

Olaf laughed happily and immediately stopped attempting to drown Jorkden. Zaria reached up to her neck to pull off the necklace, but Olaf didn't slow at her; he raced past her to the elk. Zaria dropped her arms, confused.

"What are you doing?" she asked.

Olaf stroked the white pelt with delight. The elk reared back with an awful bugle of alarm. He pranced away from Olaf, but didn't get far as Olaf snared him with a collar made of ice.

"That's not the heart," Zaria said.

Olaf laughed. "Silly, Princess. The Hart be the next Stag Lord of the ellefolken. With him in my possession, they and the elves be not stopping what comes next."

"No wait," Zaria said, rushing forward. Olaf froze her feet in place.

"No take backsies. I be taking the Hart of Gloomwood Forest," he said firmly. Then he clipped a harness on the elk.

"You tricked me," Zaria accused, eyes welling with unshed tears. "I would never have agreed to a bargain where I had to trade one innocent life for another."

"Tricked, Princess? You made your choices. Don't blame me for the outcomes of them. Your friend be freed, and you will be too once we be safely gone."

The river parted then and a hole appeared. The stag grappled mightily with Olaf, but was no match for the troll. The journey had sapped too much of his strength. Zaria sobbed. She didn't understand, but knew this was wrong. She'd made another horrible mistake.

When the elk and the troll vanished from sight, the river closed over the hole and was gone. Zaria's feet loosed and she half-ran half-stumbled to her friends on the bank. She barely heard the mountain-trolls renewed struggle for their freedom.

Aleks opened his arms as she neared and Zaria collapsed into them sobbing. The friends hugged tightly. Zaria blubbered incoherently until Filip shook her.

"Enough," he said kindly. "We can't understand you."

"This is… this is awful," Zaria cried. Her violet eyes and nose were red from her hysterics.

"I should have realized it sooner," Aleks said, taking the blame. "My dad and I go hunting all the time. Bucks, harts, bulls, stags – these are all names for the male of the species. I should have known Olaf didn't mean a physical heart."

Geirr's attention was focused on the struggling mountain-trolls. More were regaining their feet as the ice melted or they chipped at it.

"They're breaking free," Geirr stated worriedly.

Aleks groaned. "I can hardly walk let alone run."

Zaria watched as Jorkden broke his legs out of the ice. "The ice is melting and becoming fragile. Hurry, get to the water."

"What?" Filip asked. "Why?"

"The bargain with Olaf," she explained, pushing Filip in. He fell backwards into the freezing water with a yelp. "Oops! Sorry! Hurry! Go!" she urged Aleks and Geirr.

They hopped into the river and Zaria quickly followed as Jorkden moved toward them angrily. He stopped feet from them and glowered.

"Olaf's protection might extend to you here on his river, Princess, but you won't be able to stay in it for long. We'll wait you out."

He motioned to his trolden, and they scrambled to the shoreline. There he reunited with his great bear and waited, just like he said he would. Flint colored eyes watched them, glittering with hatred. He pulled his three lieutenants over and whispered to them. Without a backward glance the three trolls melded into the forest.

Chapter Thirteen: Unleashing the Dragon

They had been standing for hours in the river's waters. At first they had tried to walk in the shallows of the river to get away, but all too soon Aleks became too tired to go further. He'd then been carried a ways by Filip and Geirr at turns. It didn't do any good. The mountain-trolls kept apace, taunting from the shoreline, until Zaria stopped and told the boys to stop.

Zaria, Filip, Geirr, and Aleks were now huddled together for warmth. Zaria's teeth chattered. She kept a wary eye on the trolls as they milled around their makeshift camp. A group had started a fire some distance from the river. The warm glow beckoned to Zaria. She wanted to reach out and touch the flames. She was so cold.

"This sucks," Filip groused, voicing everyone's thoughts. His blond hair was plastered to his forehead, his nose was bright red, and his green eyes drooped with the need for sleep.

As the temperature dropped with the sun's setting, fog crept over the water. At first nobody paid it any attention. As it grew thicker Zaria gasped in delight. Her outburst garnered the attention of her friends, and also the trolls.

Jorkden frowned at her and looked around. His eyes widened. "Get cover!" he bellowed.

Trolls scrambled, and the camp fell apart in the stampede for the tree line.

"What is going on?" Geirr asked. "Why did you gasp?"

"Norwick!" Zaria said, pointing skyward.

"Wyvern!" yelled the trolls.

Geirr and the boys looked up. Through the gloom and fog, a large and familiar shape appeared. It was Norwick and a very angry looking Hector.

Other shapes emerged and Zaria gasped again in delight. More riders came in on other wyverns. The wyverns were glorious, ranging in shades of white, grey, and brown.

Archers aimed and fired. Arrows rained down on the trolls' camp. A half a dozen trolls were wounded in the initial onslaught. None were killed. It was clear that the mounted elves were not aiming to kill but to wound.

It was not so with the trolls. Jorkden and his trolden threw their spears at the flying cavalry. One of the spears struck and the wyvern screeched in pain, tumbling end over end in the air. Zaria and the boys cringed expecting the worst. His rider, however, was skilled and confident, and pulled the wyvern out of the freefall and out of harm's way.

"Go home," Hector shouted to Jorkden and the trolls. His face a furious mask. "You know the rules. The Wild Hunt is not allowed in these woods."

"We're not leaving without the princess," Jorkden shouted.

"I won't ask again," Hector said.

"The princess is ours!"

"I'm not going with you," Zaria shouted back, crossing her arms. "So don't hold your breath."

"You don't know what she's done," Jorkden taunted.

A string of curses exploded from the troll, when Hector casually aimed and fired his rifle. The bullet deeply grazed Jorkden's arm.

"Believe me," Hector growled, lowering the weapon. "I do."

Zaria shrank, keeping her gaze lowered. The anger in Hector's voice worried her. Her mouth went dry from nervousness.

Jorkden opened his mouth and cursed again, swiftly dodging another volley of arrows from the other riders. He was fleet-footed for a troll, Zaria observed.

She watched the proceedings; her attention riveted to the trolls' dirty fighting tactics. They hurled logs, tossed pots, and climbed trees to jump at the wyverns. Geirr tugged on her arm. She looked at him. He pointed to their feet.

"Grab rocks," he said, bending over to grab a handful.

Zaria didn't want to stick her hands in the cold water, but did it anyway. Filip gave Aleks an armful and reached back into the water for more.

"Aim as best as you can," Filip told her with a wink.

The boys hurled the rocks with force. Their added distraction helped the riders. With trolls ducking in one direction from the children, the elves were able to aim at them in such a way that the trolls couldn't recover and dodge in the other. They dropped like flies, clutching arms, legs, and their sides. Their howls of outrage filled the clearing.

"Children," Hector called. He and three other riders landed in the middle of the camp. "Hurry!"

Zaria and the boys dropped their rocks. Geirr and Filip shoved their shoulders under Aleks' arms and ran as fast as they could toward the wyverns. Zaria hesitated a fraction of a second then followed.

Hector pulled Aleks up onto Norwick and took off. Geirr and Filip went with two of the riders as Zaria hurried over to the last.

The rider was a tough looking female with skin the color of bark. The woman was reserved and didn't look at Zaria. She hauled Zaria up with an iron grip and launched her wyvern into the air without a word.

Zaria clung to her, unable to enjoy the flight, knowing she would be in trouble when they landed. Hector was the current Stag Lord and she was fairly certain she'd just traded his son's life for her friend's. There could be no forgiveness for an action like that.

***

Learning the consequences of one's actions was not pleasant, especially when the results were bad. The minute Zaria landed in the elves' silver clearing Hector hauled her off the wyvern and stood her in front of him. His eyes blazed with fire. He scared her.

"I'm sorry!" she wailed, not waiting for him to speak, her face crumpling.

"Don't cry," Hector said, the fierceness in his face softening slightly. "Tell me what happened. How did Hart end up in Olaf's control?"

"Hey!" Filip yelled, rushing over. "Leave her alone!" He stood between Zaria and Hector.

Zaria sucked in a deep breath, willing her eyes to stop watering. There was nothing worse than crying when you didn't want to cry. "I didn't know Hart was the elk. I thought Olaf meant the shape." She made the shape with her fingers.

Hector motioned for Filip to move aside. "Zaria, I need to know what happened. It's important. Don't spare any details."

"Olaf would only release my friend for the Hart of Gloomwood Forest."

"Good Lord," Hector breathed, his eyes widening in understanding. "So my Hart was the target all along."

"Hart?" Filip asked, confused. "The elk? Yours?"

"He's my son," Hector said, grimly, confirming for Zaria what she had suspected.

"But he's an elk!" Filip interjected. "How can he be your son?"

"Hakon will have to be informed," Hector said to himself, ignoring Filip. "This will change things."

"How is an elk your son?"

Hector looked up, catching Filip's gaze than Zaria's. "Ellefolken – elk-folk. You children have no idea the predicament you've put us in. None. Tensions were high before, but now… Damn."

Zaria bit her lip. "Tell me. I can make it right."

Hector laughed hollowly. "Oh Princess, you are kind to think it, but this will be for the elves and ellefolken to decide. We are the guardians after all."

By then Geirr and Aleks had hobbled-slash-hopped over. Geirr panted heavily under Aleks' weight.

"You need to lose weight," he complained.

Aleks whacked him on the head. "You need to work out more."

"Guardians of Queen Helena's realm?" Zaria asked.

Hector nodded, grabbed Zaria by the arm and marched her to Edevart's and Frida's home. The boys followed. The looks on their hosts' faces were grim. Hector shut the door as the children arranged themselves at the table.

"We heard the news," Edevart said quietly. He gripped Hector's shoulder in commiseration. "We will get Hart back."

"Thank you, friend," Hector said. He pulled out a chair and sat in it heavily.

The weight of the world seemed to weigh on him. Zaria felt awful. She sniffled and clutched at the necklace she was still wearing. Hector's gaze burned brightly. He leaned forward and snatched it up.

"You have the necklace," Hector said with a laugh. "Princess, I believe all is not lost. Give it to me."

Zaria undid the knot and handed it over. She was happy to learn she did something right in this mess.

"I thought this necklace was what Olaf was after, Hector," she said with regret.

"It isn't," Hector said, carefully securing the necklace around his neck. "But it's linked to Hart and will lead me to him. I can do the rest."

"Why does Olaf want your son?" Filip asked.

Frida answered for Hector. "Because, without Hart, Hector cannot reinforce Helena's realm."

At their puzzled looks, Hector explained. "The elves guard the river to ensure nobody crosses in and out of Helena's realm. It is the most obvious way into the realm, but it is not the only.

"The kings of the ellefolken are the barriers of Helena's realm. Our females can change their shape at will. They can be being, elk, or tree as it suits them.

"The males of our species are few. There is always a king, an heir-apparent, and the spare. As males we can change our shape but once.

"We start out as elks and grow to adulthood in the glade of the Golden Kings, surrounded by our fathers, grandfathers, and great-grandfathers."

"The circle of trees are the ellefolken kings," Zaria said putting it together. The hidden faces in the bark made so much more sense.

Hector nodded. "Yes. The glade is the safest space to raise the males. The protection of the other males makes it impenetrable to those who seek to disrupt Helena's realm."

"Why would losing Hart disrupt Helena's realm?"

"Our roots anchor her realm. The kings of present and past work together to secure the realm and hold it in place. We are the foundation of the Under Realm."

"Is that what you meant when you said as king you wouldn't have freedom?" Aleks asked, his eyes troubled.

Hector sighed. "Yes, it is what I meant. I will be stuck in place forever. I may watch the others live but I will be separated from it ever after."

"That's so sad," Zaria whispered.

Hector stood and took off his cloak. He hung it on a peg and sat back down. "I never looked forward to it. I had hoped to stay in this form for many more years. Hart wasn't happy about it, for he couldn't change forms until I did. I regret our last argument about it."

Frida touched his hair and moved around him to make a tea service. "Your son knows you love him. We will all work to rescue him. Do not doubt it."

"He knew better. In our elk form we are not to leave the protection of the glade unless under dire circumstances."

Zaria gulped. "I might have implied that my circumstances were dire."

Hector rubbed his neck tiredly. "The complications involved will be tremendous. The implications are unfathomable. What exactly is Olaf up to?"

"Something about coal," Geirr offered.

Edevart plopped heavily into a chair. "No!"

"How bad is that?" Aleks asked, stretching out his leg with a grimace.

Edevart noticed and hopped back out of his chair bustling around for a bowl of water and a rag. Everyone watched him, not talking until he sat at Aleks' feet and started to tend him.

"Koll," Hector said gravely, "Is the first dragon. His name literally translates to darkness. If Olaf seeks to free him, the dangers we face have just increased greatly. And Olaf now has one piece of the puzzle. Hart."

"And Helena's shoes?" Zaria asked.

"Another part," Edevart said, wrapping Aleks' leg in clean bandages. "You're fine," he told Aleks and stood to clean up.

Zaria bit her lip, worrying it. "How many parts?"

"Four," Hector said. "Taking Hart cripples the ellefolken because I will not be able to take my place by my father in the circle. If there is rotting I will not be able to shore up defenses. I will not be able to reverse the rotting. The corruption will spread, taking out the Golden Kings one at a time until the Under Realm collapses."

"What are the other two parts?" Filip said, standing to pace. He got in Frida's way, and she pressed him into helping her serve the others.

"The Drakeland Sword. Olaf will need it to break Koll's chains before the Under Realm collapses, or theoretically Koll will be crushed in the void with the others. And you, Princess," Hector said.

"Me?"

"It was supposed to remain a secret until you came into your powers, but we can't afford to keep you in the dark any longer. You must remain safe."

Zaria kept her gaze firmly trained on Hector with a feeling she already knew the answer. “Who’s my mother?”

“Queen Helena.”

Chapter Fourteen: Reuniting with Families

Hector and the three riders from before took them home. Zaria was of conflicting emotions. She wanted to stay and undo the damage her choices had caused, she wanted to go home and hug her parents tightly, and she wanted to see Christoffer to know he was safe.

From Norwick's back she watched as the miles sailed by. The struggle to get north contrasted sharply with the smooth sailing on their journey south. It was impossible to imagine that it was midnight on Saturday and that by the time they were home it would be Sunday morning. The week had flown.

“Down there,” Hector said, pointing.

Zaria followed his finger and saw the first lights of Fredrikstad. Hector motioned to the others and they started their descent. Zaria strained her gaze to see if anything or anyone was moving.

The wind whipped at her face and hair, sending her braids flying. She worried that her parents knew of her adventure. She was in so much trouble already, and she didn't want any more.

Hector harrumphed. “It looks like the stargazer held. Remarkable. I wonder who crafted it because they generally do not hold up this well.”

Zaria looked and saw the city. Unmoving cars with headlights snaked around the streets. It looked like a massive traffic jam, except the noises one would associate with a city were absent.

“That's good isn't it?” she asked after a beat.

Hector shrugged. “I don't know. Ellefolken do not play with time. Its power is not meant to be this strong. The further you travel from the place you set it the quicker time should have snapped back into place."

He steered Norwick after the wyvern carrying Aleks and his rider. They were still following Aleks' innate navigational sense. Not for the first time, Zaria wondered how he did it.

She almost asked Hector, but decided not to as it was a very personal matter for Aleks. Maybe he didn't want to know where he came from. Maybe knowing his grandmother was a changeling too was enough for him.

A part of Zaria agreed with that thinking. She wanted to know her birth mother. But she wanted to know the story behind Helena more than she wanted to meet her. It was answers Zaria sought now, not a face-to-face.

For instance, how did one become the ruler of the Under Realm? Helena was a sorceress, did that mean Zaria was too? Hector mentioned something about Zaria coming into her powers. What kind of powers would she have? Who was her birth father? Were her birth parents still together? And, finally, why did Helena (and her birth father) give her up for adoption?

Aleks' wyvern banked again and they followed, with Filip and Geirr right behind. Together they spiraled down and landed in the street in front of Filip's house. Not even the wind moved down here. The trees and branches were still.

"I can't believe we were here just six days ago," Aleks said, sliding off his wyvern, a big gray beast.

"Me neither," Geirr said, stretching his limbs. "I can't wait to get inside and take a hot shower."

"Ladies first," Zaria joked, accepting Hector's hand in getting down.

He walked them to the front door of the building. Filip grabbed the key from its hiding place and unlocked the door. As they were walking inside, Hector caught Zaria's arm and held her back.

"Remember who you are, Princess," he told her.

Zaria's forehead puckered. She stared at him in confusion. "What?"

"Remember dragons will seek to muddle you. Their power lies in deceit, fabrication, and lies."

"But you said they're all captured."

"And Olaf seeks to free the darkest and most vile one from captivity. Protect yourself and your friends. Do not trust strangers."

"Will you send word if you rescue, Hart?"

Hector nodded. "I will send word. Be safe, Princess."

Zaria watched as Hector rejoined the others. They climbed onto the winter-wyverns and launched themselves into the air. She waited, watching until she couldn't see them anymore in the gleam of the early morning dawn. Then she turned and raced indoors. The boys had waited at the bottom of the stairs for her.

"I think I could sleep for a week," Filip said, cracking a yawn.

"Well first we should shower and undo the stargazer," Aleks said. "Then call at Christoffer's and see if he made it home."

They agreed that this was the best plan and hurried the rest of the way up the stairs. Zaria plowed into the back of Filip and would have nearly tumbled back down the stairs, except for his quick reflexes. There leaning against the door jamb to Filip's room was Christoffer.

"What took you so long?" Christoffer asked.

They stared at him agog. He looked fine. His hair was freshly showered, his clothes a bit large as they were borrowed from Filip's closet.

"Jeez," Christoffer complained. "Stop staring at me like you've seen the Ghost of Christmas Past."

"You're all right!" Geirr shouted, recovering first. He launched himself at Christoffer and tackled him to the ground.

Aleks and Filip ran over and joined the roughhousing. They were laughing and joking and talking all over one another. Zaria smiled watching them. If she was honest with herself, she was feeling a little left out.

"Get over here," Filip called to her, waving an arm.

A real smile lit her features, and she ran to the boys, accepting the group hug and returning it. They were her best friends.

"Glad you're home," Zaria said, bumping shoulders with Christoffer.

"You're never going to believe what we went through to rescue you," Geirr started.

"Oh, I don't know," Christoffer said mildly. "A river-troll named Olaf held me captive in a bubble room underwater without any visible exits until about six hours ago. I might have a few stories of my own. Try me."

Aleks laughed. "Well, it started when Zaria told you about a troll you refused to believe existed. Come on man, what were you thinking? I'm a changeling."

Christoffer ducked his head. At his sheepish expression, Aleks rolled his eyes.

"Never mind. Don't tell us. You're an idiot."

Christoffer nodded. "Yes, idiot. When I saw him I thought I could bargain with him, but he wouldn't bite."

"That's because you weren't what he wanted," Zaria said kindly. "He wanted me to steal something he couldn't get close to."

"What was it?"

Zaria told him. The others filled in as she went. Christoffer was incredulous and serious by turns as the story developed. He whistled at their meeting with Norwick, groaned when they were captured by the mountain-trolls, and whooped at the story of their escape from underground.

"Oh man," he complained. "I missed everything. I would kill to see Norwick up close."

"That's only the half of it," Zaria informed him.

"There's more?"

"Lots."

They talked through the night. Conversation was grim at the news of Hart and what Olaf planned to do to release Koll. Filip was gung-ho to join the rescue mission. Zaria was too for that matter. But the practicality of it was impossible. Besides Hector had told her to stay and not do anything foolish.

On Monday morning, Aleks pulled out the stargazer and held it aloft. The egg had a reddish glow. With his finger he reached into the littlest star and grimaced. When he withdrew his hand, he shook it out.

"That was freaking hot," he muttered.

"We had it going a long time," Filip said unconcerned. "Probably meant to get that hot."

"Did it work?" Zaria asked. "Or er… stop working?"

Aleks went to Filip's window and thrust it open. He looked outside and nodded. Through the window a loud argument could be heard.

"You're so lazy, Dan, you didn't get anything done at all this weekend."

"This whole week has gone by really quickly. There just wasn't time."

"Oh yeah? Where does the time go?" the unnamed woman demanded.

A knock sounded on the door of Filip's bedroom, startling the group. Aleks shut the window.

"How's everyone doing in there?" asked Mrs. Storstrand. "School is in an hour. It's time to get up."

Her eyes went wide at seeing Christoffer and she flung the door open. "Christoffer Johansen!"

Christoffer waved. "Hi, Mrs. Storstrand."

"Your mother is worried sick about you. Where have you been?" she hustled over and gave him a bear hug. She pulled back to look at him. "Come with me, mister, we're going to go call your parents."

As she shuffled off with him, Christoffer turned back and waved. The smile on his face was wide and big. He did not mind the fuss Filip's mother was causing at all. He even hugged her back.

Epilogue: Where a Mouse Becomes a Lion

For a week Zaria was listless and edgy. She was relieved to have rescued Christoffer and that he was unharmed. At times she marveled that Olaf had kept his word. Despite the successful rescue, Zaria felt dreadful.

She'd traded one person for another and in the process had started a series of events that if left unchecked would release a dragon back into the world. She didn't know how bad it could get, but it would certainly be bad if people would be influenced against their will to do horrible things. She wondered what Olaf's and Koll's eventual game plan really was.

As for the rest of the friends, Aleks, Geirr, and Filip were fine. Their parents' hadn't noticed anything. Zaria's hadn't either. She tried not to look guilty when her mother shook her head over events that happened last week. Apparently the adults knew they did stuff, but couldn't remember any of it.

Christoffer wasn't grounded per se, but he certainly wasn't allowed out anywhere without his mom or dad. Zhuang and Emma Johansen were happy to have his friends over, but they wouldn't let Christoffer go to his friends' homes. They were focused on family bonding times. What hurt the most was to see the vulnerability in his parents' eyes Christoffer admitted one day at school.

"I hate it, but what can I tell them? That I was kidnapped by a troll? Get real."

"My parents didn't believe me when I told them about Olaf."

Christoffer slung an arm around her shoulder. "Just promise me one thing," he said.

Zaria looked at him. "Anything."

"Take me with you on the next adventure."

"The next adventure?"

"Oh come on," he teased. "We got a bad guy working to release an even bigger bad guy. There's going to be another adventure. I want in and this time around I don't want to be held for ransom."

"Can't make any promises," Zaria said, kicking at her feet. "I don't know when or if I'll be needed."

"You're a part of this fairy tale," Christoffer said with all seriousness. "You're the daughter of the Queen of the Under Realm. And you got powers." He raised his fingers and waggled them at her. "Ooooooo."

Zaria laughed and shoved him away. "Okay. Yes, the next adventure you can be the number one sidekick. Happy?"

Christoffer relaxed. "No, but I'll get there."

Zaria laid a comforting hand on his arm. "We all will."

"I thought you weren't going to make promises?"

A look of steel entered Zaria's eyes. She stood a little straighter and flipped her braids behind her shoulder. "All fairy tales have to have a happy ending. I may not be one yet, but I am going to be a dragon slayer before this is all over."

The Adventure Continues

Zaria Fierce and the Enchanted Drakeland Sword

Get a sneak peek of the next book in the Zaria Fierce Trilogy at http://keiragillett.com/drakeland-sword

About the Author: Keira Gillett

Keira Gillett is a technical publications librarian, book blogger, world traveler, artist, and now author. She graduated from the University of Florida with a Bachelor of Arts in Drawing and Painting. From an early age her mother instilled a love of the written word, as such she has always been an avid reader. She's excited to share her love of reading and Zaria Fierce with the world.

Find her at http://keiragillett.com/

About the Artist: Eoghan Kerrigan

Eoghan Kerrigan is an illustrator from Kildare, Ireland who draws primarily fantasy characters and creatures. He studied illustration in Ballyfermot College of Further Education and has produced work for various independent projects. He has two cats and a soft spot for trolls.

Find him at http://eoghankerrigan.blogspot.ie/

Made in the USA
Lexington, KY
11 June 2019